GREYSTONE HOUSE
EDITIONS

Γένοιτο

BOCCACCIO'S BONEYARD

Tales of Dread, Mystery & Sorrow

by Malcolm Greystone

McAllen, Texas

ISBN: 979-8-9951269-1-1
Library of Congress Control Number: 2026906139
Published by Greystone House Editions – McAllen, Texas
Printed in the United States of America

For the storytellers who shaped my path,
for my children, who nudged me along,
and for my wife, whose faith in me never wavered.

It is not so much what we dread at night,
as that which haunts us at morning's light.

~ The Hermit

TABLE OF CONTENTS

INTRODUCTION

The material in this book is the product of six decades of living, learning, stumbling, rising, and a lifelong urge to leave behind an artistic footprint that might outlast its maker. Like Rome, it was not built in a day. If anything, the inspiration I hoped for lagged my designs, and the work never took flight without its share of doubt. Rod Serling once remarked that writers are born, not made—a discouraging thought for anyone still perched on the edge of the nest.

There were hints of a talent, of course: the time a high-school teacher held up one of my compositions as an example to the class; or when colleagues praised my contributions to a library newsletter. But these moments were hardly an epiphany. It was not until retirement—and the strange, suspended world of a global pandemic—that the writing impulse finally took hold. I am hardly the first to find creativity in catastrophe, mind you. Did not Boccaccio produce his finest work during a plague? What about Marcus Aurelius, Procopius, Montaigne, Defoe, Cather, Porter...? History is full of writers who found their voice while the world burned. Something about widespread calamity seems to coax stories from the shadows.

As for my predilection for horror, I suspect it was preordained. Like many children, I read comic books of every stripe, from juvenile adventure to the pantheon of superheroes descended from Hugo Hercules. But it was the frightening ones —the eerie, the uncanny, the grotesque—that called me back again and again. William F. Nolan once suggested that horror fiction allows us to transcend our primal fears and emerge triumphant, better prepared for the real horrors life serves up. I believe he was on to something.

Influences and Inspirations

My teen years were shaped by a particular strain of television: science fiction, suspense, mystery, and the deliciously macabre. My staples were The Twilight Zone, The Outer Limits, The Alfred Hitchcock Hour, Dark Shadows, The Night Gallery, Kolchak: The Night Stalker, Orson Welles' Great Mysteries, Journey to the Unknown.

Cinema left its mark as well: Dracula (1931), The Picture of Dorian Gray (1945), Creature from the Black Lagoon (1954), The Time Machine (1960), Psycho (1960), The Exorcist (1973), Jaws (1975), Alien (1979); later The Mothman Prophecies (2002), The VVitch (2015), and The Wind (2018).

Reading was always a pastime. I devoured the works of H. P. Lovecraft, Clark Ashton Smith, and Horacio Quiroga. When not flipping through the pages of DC Comics' *Swamp Thing* or *House of Mystery*, I got my chills from *Tradiciones y Leyendas de la Colonia* and *El Monje Loco*, Mexican Golden Age horror magazines. Their dark stories and macabre illustrations— especially those by rare guest artists—instilled an atmosphere of dread and wonder I have never forgotten.

As adulthood settled in, my tastes broadened. I found myself drawn to the classical masters: Washington Irving, Nathaniel Hawthorne, Edgar Allan Poe, Gustavo Adolfo Bécquer, Ambrose Bierce, and H. G. Wells. My narrative essay *I Write, Therefore I Am,* included in this volume, is a nod to Irving's *Mutability of Literature* and *Westminster Abbey.* It is, in many ways, the keystone of my creative output—tamer than most of the stories here, but the spiritual grandfather of them all.

With the advent of personal computers, video game consoles and VR platforms, the influence of technology was inevitable. I caught the wave early with Myst (1993), The Seventh Guest (1993) and Phantasmagoria (1995). Later came Until Dawn (2015), Dead Secret (2015), and Dead Secret Circle (2018)—all effective in setting the mood for creative writing.

About the Title

One of the most challenging tasks in making a book—many authors will agree—is choosing a title worthy of it. Not just any title, but the one that sings, that entices, that crowns the work like a jewel on a kingly scepter. For this book, I wanted something time-worn, seemingly forgotten, a title that felt as though it belonged on the cover of a moldering manuscript—discovered, perhaps, beneath the floorboards of an old monastery.

A title that felt resurrected.

As far as anyone knows, I live in a small cave on remote Henderson Island, an abandoned mineshaft in the barrens of British Columbia, or a tree house draped in Spanish moss deep in the Atchafalaya swamp. In a literary sense, I do. My title had to evoke that feeling: one of a hermit, scratching his musings on parchment by candlelight, half in meditation, half in defiance.

Or better yet: one of a *renegade ghostwriter.* The title would convince a reader that Boccaccio himself could have authored these pages, following a bout of plague and a wild ride in Doc Brown's DeLorean—something he would have quietly hidden upon reflection, fearing it might doom *The Decameron.*

In short, I chose a title that felt medieval yet mischievous, solemn yet sly. One that ribbed its invitation; that beckoned the reader into the ossuary with a boney finger and a toothy grin.

About the Stories

I will not spoil the tales that follow. The brief descriptions below exist only to provide context, not revelation. Most are easy reads, but if one or two stories seem a bit wordy, it is only because I love language. Words are to writing what oils are to painting, and I rarely paint in monochrome.

A brief warning: this is a horror collection. Some of the stories contain graphic content, obscenity or lewdness, though sparingly compared to the more "generous" authors of our time. Sensitive readers should tread carefully with *As Luck Will Have It, The Bag, The Toadfish, Dead Men Don't Cry* and *Storytime.* Consider this your one and only caution. Look before you leap.

As Luck Will Have It — A drifter finds work—and horror—in a desert mining town. A tale that treads the line between reality and illusion, reason and madness.

The Bag — A science fiction minefield of suspense and horror, inspired by the alleged Kelly-Hopkinsville encounter.

Creeper — A lone hiker. A stalker. A strange revelation.

The Toadfish — A couple on a beach find something more than romance. A graphic, seaside plunge into modern horror.

I Write, Therefore I Am — A twist on Descartes's iconic phrase. A Gothic-style narrative essay with roots in nineteenth-century American literature.

Dead Men Don't Cry — A genius with a wicked plan confronts his own humanity. A challenging piece for readers with an interest in quantum physics and cosmology.

Knock Knock — We reap what we sow, the saying goes. Sometimes more than we harvest. From seed to catastrophic misfortune, a tale of endless heartache.

Storytime — Five youths around a campfire, all having fun. Four of them at least. A collection of outrageous and ludicrous mini-tales wrapped in a frame story.

The Hippie House — An old house. A young boy. A Hoosier's brief excursion into the painful, paranormal, and poignant.

U-47 — A German U-boat captain's ominous mission. A supernatural tale of lingering dread and maritime tragedy, written with respect for those lost at sea.

Vanity — A strange tale about self-love gone awry. A haunting parody of Oscar Wilde's *The Picture of Dorian Gray*.

Dark Matters — Some books open doors. Others eat us alive.

The 13th Story — Some people don't need a blindfold to stay in the dark. A monologue on the absurdity of self-righteousness.

A Final Words

My hope is simple: that these stories enthrall, unsettle, amuse, disturb, and delight in equal measure. I do not expect to please everyone. If even a fraction of readers find resonance here, I will consider that a triumph.

One last note: the stories in this book are entirely my own. AI played no role in their creation, though I did enlist its help in editing—just as one might consult a human editor. AI is a tool, not a muse. I would never relinquish authorship to it; doing so would diminish the very impulse that drove me to write in the first place. With that said, I hope you find this collection a worthy companion—perhaps one you will even read on a dark and stormy night.

Enjoy.

Malcolm Greystone

PREFACE

In the autumn of nineteen-eighty-one, at the unripe age of eighteen, a cousin of mine passed away. I couldn't attend his funeral for reasons beyond my control, but the whispers reached me soon enough. During the wake, as the mourners settled into prayer, a large candle beside the casket jumped—not fell—from its holder and clattered loudly to the floor. To many present, this was proof of the afterlife—because what else could it be.

Whether phantom or physics, we can at least agree on this: it must've been hair-raising to witness. And let's be honest—we've all been there. When the unforeseen gave us a jump. When the inexplicable left us woolly-minded. Sometimes we laughed.

With no other purpose have I crafted these tales. Not to shock or disturb for pleasure's sake, but to provide the reader a kind of "sweet spot" for jarring emotions; an avenue for escape within boundaries. It's the same reason thrill-seekers take to the zip-line or bungee-cord, surfboard or parachute. The danger is there. We know it. But we embrace it for the excitement, the adrenaline rush, the feather in our cap. Maybe it's nothing more than a delicious trip down memory lane, echoing the time we outran the mastodon or eluded the saber-toothed cat. Safety was only a palate cleanser.

Somewhere along the way, we discovered that fear, in small and measured doses, could be its own kind of pleasure—a rehearsal for danger, a pressure valve, a way to test the hinges of our courage without paying the full price. Stories became the proving ground, a place where the stakes felt real even when the threat was not, and where dread and delight could shake hands without either one winning outright.

The old circuitry still hums under the skin, waiting for a rustle in the dark or a creak in the hallway to remind us who we are. Not to torment, but to awaken that ancient spark—the quickened breath, the sharpened senses, the instinct that once kept us alive. And perhaps that's why we return to tales like these: to let those buried reflexes stretch, flex, and remember themselves in a place where the danger is only borrowed. Sometimes fear can be fun, and if the uneasy smile means going the mile...

Γένοιτο—Let it be.

As Luck Will Have It

There are nights when I lie awake and wonder whether a man ever truly knows where he is going, or if he merely stumbles through life like a traveler on an unlit road, trusting the ground beneath his feet not to give way. I once believed things were solid—purpose, identity, the architecture of the human soul. But time erodes certainties, wearing them down like stones in a riverbed.

People speak of destiny as though it were fixed; a star by which we navigate. Yet fate, as I have come to understand it, is less a point in the sky than a shadow: it angles, it shifts, it follows without definite form, sometimes overtaking us. Where does it leave me?

I move among others as any man might—nodding at strangers, echoing their small talk, pretending that my reflection in a window is the same one the world sees. But beneath that veneer of normalcy, something stirs—faint as the flutter of membranous wings in the attic of a long-deserted house. A nameless, perhaps even menacing truth. One that eludes introspection.

Boccaccio's Boneyard

If you crossed my path, you would notice nothing amiss. No tremor in my hands. No wildness in my eyes. Yet you might feel uneasy, as though you had brushed against something unfamiliar —something you would rather not be near. And if you lingered in that feeling long enough, if you allowed its coils to tighten, you might find yourself asking the same question that haunts me in the hours before daylight:

Who is this creature?

Is a man the sum of his joys and miseries? If so, then I am a walking elegy, stitched together from small comforts and long regrets.

Is he the sum of his desires? If so, then I am a monster, for I harbor an urge I dare not name. A craving for something forbidden.

But where were these feelings born? I cannot say with certainty, but if I had to choose, I would name Desolado—a remote mining town in the desert hills of Presidio County, north of the big river, around the time those horrible things began to happen, the lurid accounts of which are still whispered by the quaint and leery townsfolk.

Their ranks are dwindling now—the last steely remnants of a town in decay. Old-timers whose only reason for telling the story is to keep it simple and straight; unadulterated. Others will dress it up for effect, trying to breathe life into what has become, over the years, little more than a scrappy legend. Perhaps they mean to preserve it, but more likely spin their yarns with no other aim than to captivate and horrify the innocent mind—distortions of the truth notwithstanding. Yet what is truth, really, if not what we choose to believe?

What I will share with you now began on the day the McNolan kid went missing—a boy of nine or ten who ran off into the bush one morning with his old coonhound and a slingshot. His mission, some have guessed, was to track down and dispatch whatever nameless varmint had ransacked his mother's chicken coop. Something no one had told him to do.

So when the dog returned home hours later—alone, bloody, and agitated—the mother went hysterical. Her heartrending wails, they say, carried far into the hills. It is not difficult to imagine her desolation as she waited for news of her only child.

Nor did she wait long.

The search party found the brave little man, slung over the branch of an old mesquite in a canyon thick with catclaw, whitethorn and prickly pear. The mother was not permitted to see the remains.

Of the condition of the body, when it was finally brought to me, I will say only this: a casket seemed superfluous. But I had a job to perform. Preparations for burial were in order.

Some of us had fallen on difficult times because of the economic slump and soaring unemployment, and any job that put food on the table was an opportunity most Okies, as we were collectively dubbed, could not pass up. So despite my better leanings, I took on the grim task of preparing the deceased for their final destination.

Wages were slim at the mortuary, but they would suffice, and in that role I learned to clean, disinfect, eviscerate, suture, and groom the subjects of my labor. I took my work seriously, and the quality of my efforts was exemplary. But the noxious liquids used for embalming—chloral hydrate, sodium arsenate, formaldehyde, camphor, methanol—were a bane to me. They brought headaches, nausea, and I suspect hallucinations. Fear for my health was so intense that I often balked at preparing the dreadful mix. It should come as no surprise, then, that my reluctance earned me a demerit—courtesy of the senior mortician, Mr. Graves, under whose perennial scrutiny I labored. The irony of his name was discomfiting, no doubt, and perhaps had shaped his character, for the man's heart was a hollow trench, and he refused to make concessions. Yet the director of the establishment, Mr. Eikenberry—an old-world import of hawkish appearance and unusual manner—was more sympathetic. When he learned of my problem, he made certain changes. He spared me the duties I loathed, assigning me those more innocuous which were still important to business. This was done over my colleague's objections, as it meant he alone would be in charge of the preservation. But Eikenberry's decision was final. I thought it was fair and appropriate, though Graves had a hard time adjusting.

Be that as it may, I continued to work in a place where exposure to hazardous materials was an ongoing risk; and partly for that reason, or perhaps entirely because of it, I would eventually quit. But until that day, I carried out my duties with diligence, even assisting Graves in other capacities.

Because of my limited income, I had taken up residence in an old two-story building nearby—a frontier jailhouse which had seen new life as a boarding lodge for migrant workers when the silver mines opened, but was vacant within a year due to problems sourcing water. Before it was shuttered, however, its new owners had it restored, and even called it home for a time, adding various inducements to attract future leaseholders. When they found another place to live, they offered me accommodations there, on the condition that I pay rent on time and manage the dwelling responsibly. I accepted, and a contract was formalized.

The front door creaked as I entered the house, and before long I found myself standing in a spacious parlor. There, a large mirror with an intricately carved wooden frame hung on the far-side wall. I was not fond of this fixture, given its obnoxious habit of surprising the unwary resident with a mock twin in a house with no other occupants. But there it was.

Despite the incommodity, there was much to admire in this room: the hand-woven rugs, the brass ornamentation, the stylish furniture—all neatly arranged and purposely seductive. This was the main living area, though I rarely spent time in it.

Moving on, I inspected the kitchen and dining room, and beyond these a pair of modest bunk rooms—former detention cells, as it came to mind. I seldom spent time in these either.

Upstairs I found six more bunk rooms, equally small. They were mostly empty but for some bed frames, boxes, and carpenter tools, from which I inferred their state of restorative paralysis. But the ceilings were tall and the floorboards solid, so I made one of these my living quarters, preferring it to my ground-level options for the external views it afforded. The windows, by the way, with their wrought-iron bars, lent the house that rustic feel of a nineteenth-century crowbar hotel—so to speak—and though the fear of getting trapped in a blaze was never absent, few things in that dwelling could actually be set aflame.

Boccaccio's Boneyard

Behind the house was a more recent annex: a small conservatory or sun room—very plain in construction, with glass doors that framed a rear-side landscape. Out there, a derelict stable bemoaned its own wretchedness; a crippled fence guarded what once had been a corral; a spindly water tower—its rusted hoops and wooden staves mostly in place—groaned miserably under the weight of its years.

Off to the side of these tottering structures was an old-fashioned well with a waist-high wall crudely finished in cobblestone. Atop it lay the skeletal remains of an ancient cover, offering little protection from the elements and the occasional tumbleweed that found refuge in its throat. Even so, it was no worse for wear after countless years of neglect. In fact, I fancied, in a moment of jest, that I might find a passage to the underworld through its gaping mouth—there to confirm or debunk rumors of an eldritch race of mole-people said to inhabit the bowels of the earth. At the very least, I intended to make the real bounty in its depths accessible once more to the parched world above.

This proved more work than expected. I removed many boards, branches, and bales from its interior, noting that a few heavy bricks had fallen away from the inner lining just above the waterline. This exposed what appeared to be an infirmity in the earthen wall, resolutely patched in some ill-remembered past. But assuming the water below kept its depth, replacing the fallen bricks seemed pointless. Doing so offered little gain, and there were more important matters requiring my attention. So after much labor, I completed the project, and the cool, fresh water in the well was once again ready at the drop a bucket.

❖ ❖ ❖

Few buildings in Desolado deserved more than a passing glance. One of these was a church known by the wistfully appropriate name of Sacred Heart. Built from humble materials in the Spanish colonial vein, it baffled the keen eye with its Baroque façade and Gothic windows. Something in that odd blend of architectures appealed to me and lured me inside. It was a place for quiet reflection—a place where I could steal away and lose myself in prayer, unencumbered by the world outside. Ah, but how often we are misguided by our impulses.

The ghostly candlelight, the vivid statuary, the narcotic whiff of incense—these had a strange effect on me, almost hypnotic, and I found myself suddenly transfixed. My vision blurred, the world around me spun, and in that haze of altered consciousness I nearly overlooked the monk standing beside me, regarding me warily from the dark of his cowl. A moment later he turned away, glancing back now and then as he put distance between us. His trepidation was obvious, though the reason for it was not; and not knowing what to make of it, I waved him back. Instead, he quickened his pace and soon vanished into the shadows of the sacristy. I do not recall what happened next. I must have dozed off, for all I remember is waking to find the doors of the church unlocked, late as it was after the hours of visitation. There was water on the floor, too—little puddles and trails of it. Mostly around the baptistery, but also round about me.

As bizarre as this seemed, I chose not to linger, wasting no time getting home and out of wet clothing. I had plans to explore the town and acquaint myself with its people the following day, and I would not suffer more of this uncanny experience.

Wandering about town, I came across the market square: a place where hawkers, tradesmen, and women offering savory dishes gathered to peddle their wares and fares. The venue was a conglomerate of wooden huts, canvas tents, and jerry-built stalls where buyers rummaged for things they needed, coveted, or simply wished to inspect. And it was here, in a lonely corner of this makeshift emporium, that I discovered a little yerbería—the sort of place one might take for a shop selling herbs and spices, though it often hides a duskier trade. Naivety is the only reason one might stop here for something to flavor their soup with.

This is where I met Alonzo, a veritable sage and wellspring of knowledge who acquainted me with many legends of Old Mexico and the American Southwest. A man who sometimes procured for me—without solicitation—charms, amulets, and remedies for the various hexes or ailments I was allegedly the victim of or required protection against. I humored him, mostly to keep things friendly.

Don Alonzo, as I addressed him with the Spanish honorific given to men of age or distinction, was a codger of sorts: a lean, somewhat cagey old fellow with copper skin, drooping eyes, and wisps of white hair on his brows and chin that resembled cotton in the shade of his moth-eaten gambler. He spoke little of his past, yet possessed many "credentials," among which proficiency in the art of traditional healing was the most widely known in the region. Perhaps this is why people in those parts referred to him as *el mago, el curandero,* or simply *el doctor*—though some callous folks privately called him *el brujo.*

Alonzo knew how to spin a good yarn, but it was one very unusual tale that caught my avid ear. In it, he spoke of a certain oddity that existed in the world—an eerie outsider, yet somehow part of the natural order. A *nagual,* he called it. A mysterious element in the folklore of many cultures, it appears in old texts, turns up in ancient art, and—more unsettling still—lives in the shadows of our modern world. He said there was a belief among the indigenous peoples of the South, and elsewhere too, that each person is paired with a guiding spirit at birth—the rare and exact date of which, if unlucky, would determine who would become a nagual. Women dreaded going into labor on such days, for individuals thus marked by the ancient calendar took the form, at night, of that one thing their lives were fatefully intertwined with: a snake, an owl, a coyote, a panther—or something else entirely. People in their villages took sudden refuge in their huts, barricading doors and windows whenever word spread that a nagual was afoot, for it could be a heinous thing. A bite or scratch from such a creature, legend said, condemned its victim to a life of perdition—that is, if the victim survived at all. Even today, Alonzo said, people go to yerberías to obtain magic salts, pepper-tree sprigs, or crowns of garlic to ward off suspected naguales. And they spare no expense, for no price is too high for their safety.

"Heed my advice," the old man warned. "Should you ever find yourself looking out the window at night, do not stare long —turn away! *¡Retira la mirada!* For it lurks in the shadows, that prowling menace; an image you dare not strain to see, lest you behold it suddenly: a hideous thing with gaping jaws, eyes like burning coals—and two grisly things that are not five-legged tarantulas, but really hands!"

Alonzo paused to sign himself in a cross. Then, realizing he had overplayed the part, he offered up a half-toothless grin.

Resuming his ominous tone, he revealed something disturbing. He believed the McNolan boy had been the victim of a dire beast—a much-errant nagual, no less, which had recently migrated north of the river to make Desolado the focus of its depredations. Even more, Alonzo claimed he could identify the creature if he put his mind to it, and that he would do so very soon. Once he knew its whereabouts, he said, he would lead a posse of armed recruits to finish off the scourge before it could wreak more havoc or move on to another town.

But Alonzo's plan was premature, for he would not live to consummate his wish. That evening, shortly after nightfall, he was struck down in his hovel on the outskirts of town—alone and so remote that his cries would not spare him the violent end he met. I felt his loss for many reasons, but mostly because I realized I would never learn the secret of his reputed gift: the power to expose the ambush, *to unveil the hidden threat*—if indeed such a power existed. For how else would I avoid a similar fate?

I mourned for Alonzo.

I mourned for myself.

❖ ❖ ❖

One morning, as I cast off the shackles of a torturous dream, I glanced out my bedroom window and saw what appeared to be a dark figure standing beside the well. I tried to push the glass open, but it would not budge, resisting my attempts to hail the stranger.

Reaching the well took only a minute, but by the time I stepped outside, the figure had vanished. A dense fog had settled in the area, as though a great cloud had fallen to earth, limiting my visibility. I called out twice, but got no reply. Then it occurred to me: there were scarcely any boundaries on the property. No signs restricting passage. So trespassers came and went very much as they pleased, as did my visitor on this occasion—which would not be the last.

The bell tower soon became the focus of confusion, with people clustering in number in the street. Big, black birds circled overhead, their shadows sweeping across the onlookers, who struggled for a better view.

Suddenly, an altar boy staggered from the church, yelling, "*¡Muerto! ¡El padre está muerto!*" Several townspeople rushed to him, demanding an explanation, and the young acolyte led them inside, up a narrow flight of stairs, and onto a flat section of the roof.

Arriving ahead of their wits, those who had followed the boy froze at the sight before them. There lay the friar I had seen before: dead, as the boy had claimed. But that was not all. When the group fell upon the scene, a mob of ghoulish birds scattered abruptly, revealing a ravaged skull and pieces of a mangled corpse, strewn about the tattered remains of a blood-soaked habit. Yet horror quickly gave way to intrigue when they noticed half the body was missing—though soon it became clear why the church bell had not rung all day.

Her name was Eulalia. It was a fine name—rare, mellifluous, pulchritudinous. I told her so. My words lumbered forth like fat pigs quitting their mud wallow. She only smiled—not modestly, but with a kind of knowledge gathered from the stupid way I said it; my vain attempt to conceal my admiration. But who was to blame. Here was a woman in the flower of her youth, bred from the finest stock. Her eyes, lips, hair, skin—all of these suggested a unique constellation of bloodlines; a wonderful if obscure mixture as striking as I had ever beheld. I was drunk with her beauty, surrendering to a thirst I could not quench. And yet, for such an eyeful, she was not the least pretentious, graciously ignoring the awkward stare I often cast her way.

Eulalia was unique in many ways. For one, she was frugal with words. Not timid or aloof, but if my own life was an open book, hers was a fortress—one she defended with gentle rebuffs whenever I battered the ramparts.

As for attire, she did not follow herds. She dressed in a style reminiscent of an earlier period, favoring darker hues. This was not off-putting, but it challenged every notion I had of a woman with a taste for fashion.

Nor, as I recall, did she ever eat or drink, declining every invitation to share my table. By what means she nourished herself was something I was never made privy to, and while three meals a day were commonplace for me, Eulalia seemed perfectly well and fit without sustenance.

Then there was her odd habit of appearing unexpectedly by the well. I assumed she had a fascination for such relics—or perhaps only this one—in whose depths her attention would often get lost for minutes at a time. On one such occasion, while seemingly rapt in thought, she asked me if I was afraid.

"Afraid of what?" I asked.

With her eyes still fixed on the inky black water below, she cocked her head back, as one fishing might set the hook. This intrigued me, and when I pressed her to explain, she turned to look at me. Her eyes were two vestigial dots obscured by a layer of unbroken skin—and then were normal again. I winced at the illusion. Eulalia noticed my reaction and surprised me with a burst of laughter, dismissing the unanswered question. This was unusual, and reminded me of the way she answered when asked about her obsession with the well. She said she went there on occasion to make a wish, nothing more. A common ritual among dreamers with fragile hopes and big aspirations. A widespread practice I was surely aware of.

This was clearly a ruse to avoid disclosing what I suspected to be a deeper truth, and for the moment I was taken aback. But because I loved Eulalia, I did not pursue it.

Boccaccio's Boneyard

Eyes, ears, noses, tongues—these are precious commodities. They are the means by which we assimilate the world around us. To have them ripped from their sockets or wrenched from their moorings is an act of utter insensibility, for it renders the victim so. But the work is not complete without harvesting more of the anatomy—which was clearly the assailant's intent, and something it might have accomplished had it not beaten a hasty retreat when confronted by a pair of hunters with shotguns.

The victim was an elderly widow who had scoffed at her neighbors' warnings when she took to the street for a nighttime stroll. Their well-meant reproaches were met with a flurry of hostile rebukes and unfiltered oaths. A few small children overheard the exchange and began to cry, whereupon their parents tried to explain the altercation, impressing upon them the dangers that roam in the night, though not without loving reassurances. In time, they were put to bed; their fears extinguished. Meanwhile, in a bid to allay their own, the adults gathered to pray, reserving their best intentions for the one whose fate, unfortunately, cemented those fears.

The two men who had witnessed the attack were still at the scene when the sheriff arrived, but when questioned, neither could give a coherent description of the person or thing responsible for the atrocity. One claimed it was a large, hairy beast —brown or gray—that tore into its prey like a steak even as the men lined up their barrels. The other insisted it looked like a pale sinewy man with long limbs and a face like a rat's... or a bat's. One swore it was inhumanly swift on its legs, bolting from the scene at the peal of gunfire and leaving in its wake a swarm of hellish fireflies, as when someone rakes a bed of hot coals in the wind.

The other maintained it hissed like a snake, fell to the ground, and with its arms folded across its chest, slinked away like a sidewinder.

Neither story could be reconciled, and the sheriff, unable to make any headway, made no further attempt at inquiry, having no option but to issue the men a citation. As he later stated, not a single clue—except for that which left its trace on their breath—could be drawn from either witness.

The following day, as I was cleaning the body, the ever-vigilant Graves entered the preparation room and instructed me to halt my work. Apparently, the deceased woman was marked for cremation. I reminded Graves that if he was not going to embalm the corpse, he need not be present, and that I would gladly transfer the remains to their offsite destination. But he refused my offer and took charge of the delivery himself.

Three more attacks occurred in the weeks that followed—the victims a pair of drifters and a local con man—and in each case the perpetrator fled before anyone could intervene. The level of brutality exhibited by these attacks was not the hallmark of any animal known to frequent the area, and so it was presumed to be the work of an insanely cruel person; a theory which gained wide acceptance when it was revealed that the many traps laid out by local ranchers were left undisturbed.

It was not long before Eulalia learned of my plight. I told her of my dreams, their unpleasant nature, how they had grown worse over time, and how I feared they would break down the wall of sleep. She wondered if my job was getting the better of me, a theory I dismissed. Then she asked if a strange or unsettling story had rattled me. Annoyed, I scoffed at the notion, lambasting her in a way I soon regretted. Apologies had no effect. Eulalia's face flushed, but tears did not follow. To my surprise, she composed herself, gave me one look, and without a word walked away.

A shadow lingers o'er me now.
It came to me, I know not how.
My only hope is that I find
a harbor safe, and peace of mind.

The flesh is weak, the soul is frail.
Herbs and salts do not avail.
I near the pit—the Great Abyss!
And so I humbly ask you this:

Guard me henceforth, all my days,
and keep me faithful in your ways,
that I may suffer nevermore
the demon lurking at my door.

A poem I recall from a dream. A prayer perhaps. Who can say.

That night, as I was going to bed, I heard something crash in the house. Barefoot, I fumbled through the dark, moving through rooms and hallways until I reached the conservatory, where I believed the noise had originated. Cautiously, I searched for a light, when something pierced my sole. I had stepped on a shard of glass from a broken door pane.

The door was latched and there was no sign of entry, for what intruder would have locked it behind? Even so, I stayed long enough to make sure no attempt was made. I strained for a look through the broken glass, but saw nothing in the darkness beyond. So I returned to my room, dressed my foot, had a brandy, and soon fell asleep. The previous weeks had taken their toll, and I had not found much rest.

That night would be different. I had a dream, and in my dream I saw a dark figure leaning over me. I did not feel threatened. If anything, I felt peace—an odd sensation, unlike many nights previous when I found myself adrift in a sea of torments. For once, the weight of despair had lifted. I yearned for nothing. I hungered for nothing. I slept soundly that night. And yet, waking on the parlor floor the next morning was profoundly disconcerting. How I got there remains a mystery. I have no recollection of it; no idea what transpired during the night— though fragments of an image, bizarre and vaguely human, occasionally flash through my head.

The demolition crew arrived on schedule. Men in hardhats, and rumbling machines belching fumes and hungry for destruction. The owners of the house had notified me that the property had been requisitioned by the mining authority, which had begun probing the land again in a last-ditch effort to draw whatever silver remained in the earth. This happened on very short notice, and so I was forced to move out, spending time in a flop nearby while pondering my next move.

I was sorry to see the old house ravaged: a brooding colossus, boldly facing its inquisitors and their instruments of torture; proudly and contemptuously enduring the abuse; then gradually succumbing, till nothing remained but a heap of rubble.

The stable, fence, and water tower came next; but these offered little resistance as they were mere travesties of their former selves, and in any case had long awaited the inevitable.

The well came last. The cobblestones in its wall gnashed like teeth as it broke apart, and the whole thing collapsed with a sound like thunder, decimated by a mammoth contraption on steel tracks. Then a big mound of earth swept over the hole—a grave unto itself—blotting it from existence.

All that remained on the property was a rusty old mailbox languishing on a rotted post. Inside I discovered a note.

"What harm is there in darkness?" it said.

I only read it once.

Eulalia never said goodbye. I had hoped we would meet again, that I could make amends. But I knew not where to look. She never told me where she dwelt or where I might send correspondence.

It was hardly any wonder. Eulalia was a master of riddles, a guardian of secrets, a walking enigma—whatever one chooses to call her. I tried to find her, of course, looking far and wide; asking whomever I met if they had seen someone fitting her description. No one had. A few rascals offered me clues and encouraging leads, but these turned out shams. I came to embrace disappointment, faithfully waiting for me at the end of the day.

I would like to think Eulalia was more than a friend. Why am I uncertain? To that I have no answer. Yes, there were things I did not know about her and probably never would. But if two people embrace, if they linger in that moment, if their souls are like two candles touching, burning, fusing—are they yet strangers?

I assume she moved away, for I never saw her again. I would like to think she went someplace where the weather was good and the plants seldom bite. I would want her to know I was happy for her. But for me, the question wears on: was there a place in her heart for a guilt-ridden man? It would be easy to say her absence meant nothing; that I boldly moved on and never looked back. Easy, and perhaps I should—but it would be a lie.

The day before I quit my job, there was a great commotion in the streets. Whether his name was real or just an alias is a matter of debate, but a man called Fleischer—a violent and sadistic criminal who had found himself trapped in a hail of bullets—lay pale and stiff in the back of a wagon.

People in town were celebrating. Here, they claimed, was the butcher of Desolado. The man responsible for all the recent murders. Everyone knew this because he had slaughtered six people in other parts of the land—with a cleaver. But his days on the run were numbered. Acting on a tip, the authorities had tracked him to an isolated hovel near the canyons. Before slain, he had vowed to tear apart his would-be captors, "just as he had the others". The evidence was overwhelming.

The truth may never be known. The evidence, in fact, was lean. It just so happened that the carnage ended with Fleischer's demise, as the mayor was keen to point out. He said, in effect, that the nightmare was over; that no one need fear anymore, now that the beast burned in hell. He told the townsfolk precisely what they wanted to hear. The truth, as he put it.

And so the nightmare *was* over. The people had reason to rejoice, and to them that was all that mattered. For what is truth, really, if not what we choose to believe?

The men, women, and children of Desolado slept soundly that night, as they did the following night, and many a night thereafter, though the events of that year would not stray far from thought. Such memories are not easily buried.

As for Fleischer, even criminals have a place in the ground. Arrangements were made for a discreet interment, and it was I who was in charge of preparing the body—my last assignment before leaving the post. I did all that was required of me, one last time, which in Fleischer's case included the concealment of bruises, gunshot wounds, and lesions on his arms and legs like those inflicted by a vicious dog or wild animal. Mr. Graves took care of the rest; but not before we settled our differences, after which we amicably parted ways.

As for Eikenberry, with whom I had been on easy terms from the start, there is not much to say. He regretted losing his staff, but the town was dying anyway. The last time I saw him he was sitting at his desk, absent-looking—idling the time, oddly, with a slingshot he had pulled from a drawer, at one point toppling a ceramic jar from its plinth. Unimpressed, I bade him farewell and turned away, careful not to step in the old widow's ashes.

And that concludes my experience working as an assistant undertaker in the town of Desolado.

If there is one thing we can draw from all this, it is undoubtedly the fact that monsters exist. The knowledge that they live, breathe, and secretly walk among us. While some might take this literally, others have their doubts. To them, I speak of the bogeyman or *el cucuy*—evils that well-meaning parents caution their children against. To others yet, I speak of the worst of felons: pathological evildoers whose crimes are without rival. But no—what I refer to are genuine outsiders, not myths or miscreants. Not the psychotropic invention of a deluded mind. I mean they are *real*. As real as the ancient stoneware they were carved or hand-painted on. As real as the clay from which their frightful little figures are crafted for display in yerberías. As real as the ink in this journal. I should know... *for I have seen one*. In the parlor of that house where I lived, and in the well behind it, leering at me from the moonlit water below as I craned over the edge for a look.

But never mind what I say, for it is not my place to convince those who disbelieve. In fact, I must go. To what destination I cannot say. I need to keep moving, searching—always. Call it a craving if you will.

And yet, I wonder. Why must it always be so? Will I ever find a place to call home? But no. Time is always wasted, opportunities are lost, and along the way many a chance to end this miserable, wandering existence.

Who knows. It is said we have only ourselves to blame for our misfortunes, though sometimes I pause and reflect. What if everything is as it was meant to be? What if Destiny plots our course? What if, as they say, the fault is in our stars.

Ah, but here they come again... the *visions*. Thrice daily they visit me. There is no stopping it. Visions that will haunt me for the rest of my days. Of people, young and old, big and small, lying peacefully in eternal rest. Of their bodies—their flesh—once warm and supple, now cold and rigid. Changing ever so steadily into these awful, dry, leathery things that reek of... sickly, noxious preservatives.

Boccaccio's Boneyard

The Bag

Cindy had always hated the windows at night. In the daytime they were harmless—bright squares that framed the yard, the corn, the shed, the long gravel road. But after sundown, when the house lights were on and the world outside turned to ink, the glass became a mirror. You could see yourself clearly, but anything beyond your reflection was a guess, a shadow, a suggestion. Tonight, something had been looking back. She was still trembling when she confronted Harold. The living room smelled faintly of the pot roast she'd overcooked, and the television murmured in the background, but none of it grounded her. She stood in the middle of the room, arms crossed, voice sharp with anxiety.

"I'm telling you it was not an owl, Harry! I know what an owl looks like! It was not an owl! What part of *not-an-owl* do you have trouble understanding?"

Harold barely looked up from the recliner. "What else could it be? Whaddaya think it was?"

"I don't know. I just know it was not an owl. It was bigger and didn't have any feathers."

"Ya saw it in the window?"

"Right there. Peeping at me. It scared the living daylights out of me. It wasn't a person either."

"Ya had a good look?"

"Not a good look. I just know what I didn't see."

"Oh c'mon, Cindy," Harold snorted. "Listen to yerself. Ya know what ya didn't see."

"That's not how I meant it."

Harold sighed, pushing himself up from the chair. "Awright, I'll have a look."

"No! Don't go out there! What if it's dangerous? You might get hurt!"

"Relax. I won't get hurt—whatever the damn thing is. I'll have my Remington by my side."

"Shouldn't you call the police?"

"The police? The police don't come here no more, remember? Too many false alarms. Besides, why should they come? By the time they got here, yer owl—or whatever it is—will be gone."

"You don't know that."

"Neither do you, darlin'. I'm prob'ly gonna shoot somebody's dog."

Cindy's eyes widened. "Where's Jinx? My cat—where is he?"

"I dunno. Last time I heard him he was meowin' on the porch. Prob'ly wants more tuna. Where'd my shells go?"

"Your shells?"

"My shotgun shells. Okay, found 'em."

"Oh, why do I think this is a bad idea?"

"Will ya stop worryin', woman? I'll take care of it. I'll miss my show's climax, but who the hell cares."

"Please don't go."

"I'm already out the door."

The night swallowed him immediately. It was moonless, thick, the kind of darkness that felt like tar. Earlier, the crickets had been chirping—steady, rhythmic, comforting. Now they were silent. Cindy stood in the living room, pacing, wringing her hands. Every few seconds she drifted toward the door, peering left and right through the bug screen, searching for any sign of Harold.

Then a blast shattered the quiet.

Cindy froze.

Then another.

And another.

Then nothing.

Her legs thawed at once. She darted to the bedroom, yanked open the nightstand drawer, and grabbed her revolver—the one she hated; the one she swore she'd never touch. Her hands shook so badly she nearly dropped it. She returned to the living room, breath shallow, heart pounding.

"Ohhh, this is a bad dream," she whispered. "A bad, bad dream. I wish I'd wake up. Harry? Are you there? Can you hear me? Please tell me it's okay.

She called the cat next. "Jinx? Here boy! Tsk, tsk, tsk! Come to momma!"

No answer.

Then something crashed in the shed—metal on concrete, tools clattering, shelves rattling. Cindy fumbled for the phone, grabbed it, and dialed dispatch. But the line was dead. Her pulse went up a notch.

Fifteen minutes crawled by. Every sound felt amplified. Every shadow became a threat. Cindy held the revolver in both hands, arms locked and trembling. Then she heard footsteps. A shape filled the doorway.

"For God's sake, Harold! Don't do that! How many times have I told you? You're gonna give me a heart attack! Besides, I could've shot you!"

She lowered the revolver, a sigh of relief bursting from her lungs. "What happened? What took you so long? I heard shots."

Harold stepped inside. His face was gray. He clutched a plastic bag tightly to his chest. It held something round, about the size of a soccer ball. His eyes were peeled wide, glassy, as if he'd seen something that had warped his understanding of the world.

"They got old Dan Brooks," he said.

"Brooks? The guy up the road? Who got him?"

"They got poor old Dan."

"Who are *they*?"

"Those things."

"What things?"

"Those... things."

"Things! Things! What things? Can you be more specific?"

"Goblins."

"Goblins? What do you mean, goblins? What on earth are you talking about?"

"They were all over 'im. They was very strong. He... he tried to beat 'em off, but he couldn't. They was all over 'im."

"Gremlins? Are you telling me gremlins got him?"

"Not gremlins. Goblins. More like... people. People from..."

"What happened to Brooks?"

"It was horrible."

"What? What was horrible? Tell me!"

Harold swallowed hard.

"I went outside, looking fer that thing ya said. That thing ya saw in the window."

"Did you see Jinx? Where's Jinx?"

"I went outside, looking fer that thing—and I found it. Yer owl. It was a goblin. I found it, and then..."

"I heard some shots. Two or three loud ones."

"Right. There were three of 'em—at first. Two by the shed, one behind the house. They was silver-like."

"What were they? What happened? Did you shoot them?"

"I did. Shot 'em all."

"And what then? Are they still out there? Did you kill them?"

"I pump 'em with lead. Yeah, that's what I do. Pump 'em with lead. But that don't go down very well. I shot one square in the chest. It takes a tumble. Same with the other two."

"Go on."

"They get up like nothin' happened. And then they come at me, hoppin'. Hoppin' like those things at the zoo. Like kangaroos. They come hoppin' like kangaroos."

"Oh God."

"They grab me. Then more show up. They come out of the barn, out of the corn, out of the sticks. They come out and grab me. All of 'em, shiny like silver coins. I'm kickin' and punchin', but they come at me like a pack of wild dogs. Like wild dogs. I can't beat 'em off."

"Harry, what did they do? Did they hurt you? What did they do to you?"

"They take me inside this ball. This... big ball in the sticks."

"A ball?"

"A ball. Yes. In the woods. Very shiny, jus' like all of 'em. They take me inside and... Oh God... it was horrible! Jus' horrible!"

"Harry! Look at me! Get a grip of yourself! What was horrible? Look at me!"

"They strap me down. They hook me up. It's cold. They're bringin' out their tools—bringin' out their mean-lookin' tools—and all the while I'm lookin' all 'round me. I'm lookin' all 'round... and I see lots o' things. Cut-open things."

"What do you mean? What things? Cut-open how? Was Brooks there?"

"Pigs, chickens, rabbits. All cut up. Their insides taken out. Put in jars like Grandma's preserves. Like the frogs and mice we cut up in science class, remember that? We put 'em in jars."

"Oh God. You're scaring me."

"I know I'm next. They wanna cut me up. They're bringin' out their tools. They're fixin' to cut me up. They're all over me like mad bees."

"But you got away. You're here, so you got away."

"Yes. Had to get away. They was gonna put me in a jar. Couldn't let 'em."

"How did you escape?"

"Don't know. The straps come off. I'm twistin' and turnin' and I finally break free. I snatch one of their tools and stab one in the eye. They all go mad. I jump up and run. I get out fast, runnin' past all the bodies. The ones they cut up."

"And you got away! I'm so glad. You had me worried like heck. So what's in the bag?"

"Nothin'."

"Nothing? You're telling me there's nothing in that bag?"

"Goin' outside. Need to do somethin'."

"Don't change the subject, Harry. What's in the bag?"

"None of yer concern. Fertilizer."

"Fertilizer?"

"Gotta bury it. No other place for it."

"Don't lie to me, Harry! I wasn't born yesterday. Tell me what you have there. What do you have in that bag?"

"Gotta bury it. Fertilizer."

Cindy felt an odd sensation in her gut. It gathered there as though she had eaten something spoiled.

"What happened to Brooks?

Harold didn't answer. A frown came down like a curtain over his face. A moment later it rose.

"Gonna bury it now."

Wha... Harry, look at me! Look at me when I'm talking to you! What happened to Brooks?"

Harold paused. A faint tug of irony pulled at the corner of his mouth as he stared emptily into space.

"Brooks?... They took 'im. Hauled 'im off—kickin' and screamin'. Up, up, and away."

"Dear God!"

Harold turned toward the door. He looked very weak. He took a few steps, then stopped in his tracks. His arms slackened, and the bag slipped. Cindy gawked. He was bleeding from a large wound in his chest—his heart still pumping in the open cavity. He wobbled there for a second like a massive tree being felled, then crumpled to the floor, dropping his cargo, the contents of which tumbled out.

Cindy fainted.

The cat was out of the bag.

Creeper

Gina stopped at the trail head to pull up her socks and check the fit of her new hiking shoes. She was aware of the car parked in the shade some twenty paces away—and of its driver, whose unbroken stare through the open passenger window made her skin prickle. It was the reason she faced him while adjusting her footwear. She knew the lines of her body were accentuated by the shorts and halter top she wore, and she had no intention of indulging him. He'd already helped himself enough during her warm-ups. She saw no reason to whet his appetite further. Even from here, through the shifting shade and the intermittent puffs of cigarette smoke, she recognized the look: the leer of a dog at the table.

In a situation like this, a woman sensing danger would not venture alone into the wilderness. Gina was usually prepared, and what she often carried for protection against four-legged predators could easily suffice for the two-legged ones. But today was different. An oversight had left her defenseless. Even so, she didn't return to her vehicle. Confident in her athletic physique—and perhaps foolishly in the eyes of another—she pressed her luck and hit the trail.

She had planned a brisk two-hour walk through the mountain forest, aided only by the meager contents of a small backpack. Longer treks demanded time she didn't have; obligations waited for her before late afternoon.

But a brisk walk was no longer the plan. Gina launched into a full sprint, knowing that if she looked back and saw the man match her movements, her suspicions would be confirmed.

A minute into the dash, she stopped cold. Looking down the slope, she could barely make out—through dense trees and vegetation—the unmistakable shape of a man running up the winding trail at breakneck speed. Her pulse, already rapid, spiked. But she still had the edge. If she kept her wits, she could outrun or outsmart him, hiding in the woods if necessary.

A partial blessing materialized in the form of a sudden fork in the trail, splitting the odds against her. She took the lower grade, hoping to throw off her chaser, thinking he'd assume she'd continued upward to maintain the advantage of height. Either way, the craggier terrain and thickening forest would work in her favor.

But soon she regretted her choice. From the pit of her mind surfaced an unpleasant reminder: hikers in distress, for reasons unclear, statistically favored the lower path. Maybe he knew this. Was there time to double back?

Her answer struck like a punch when she came face-to-face with her pursuer. Both runners froze about thirty steps apart, locked in a surreal detente. Gina saw he was not in peak condition

—his open mouth and heavy panting gave him away. She seized on this. The moment the chase resumed, she enacted her plan: scale the escarpment beside her.

Not far into the climb, a powerful hand seized her. She screamed despite herself, but adrenaline surged, and with a solid handhold she rolled over and kicked him squarely in the face. The blow freed her. She scrambled to the top of the escarpment, struggling past the roots of a toppled tree, and put some distance between them.

Wandering through the darkening forest, Gina looked back often. For the moment, no one followed. This gave her time to reflect on her sins. What had brought her to this condition, she wondered? Was it hiking alone? Ignoring the danger? Hubris? Others took these risks without consequence. Why her?

But she knew it was more than that. She was a flower. A beautiful zinnia. A magnet for butterflies, hummingbirds—and vermin. Her looks were a gift and also a curse, and she knew which one ruled now. If she were old or plain-looking, she wouldn't have found herself in this predicament. Clearly, her beauty had its downside. But self-recrimination was a luxury she couldn't afford now. She pushed these thoughts aside and pressed forward, searching for an exit from the crisis. Then a trail came into view. A different one. Cautiously, she followed it.

An hour had passed before fatigue crept in. A twisted ankle didn't help. Carly opened her backpack to refresh herself with drink. The silence reassured her, but she couldn't shake the thought that her stalker was still out there; still on the hunt. Then she noticed it: a message on a sheet of paper, tacked on a tree.

Boccaccio's Boneyard

Apprehension rose sharply as she approached. Her eyes widened when she realized who had written it. In red marker:

"*Hello, Gorgeous,*

I know you're still around here somewhere—and just to let you know, so am I. It's just the two of us now, tucked away in this wild, lonely forest. Nice, isn't it? I've had my eye on you since the moment you stepped out of your car. Couldn't help myself. A woman like you... well, you don't just walk past a man's life without leaving a mark. So I made a promise to myself. I was going to meet you, even if it took me all day. But don't you worry, Lollipop. I'm patient. And I'm close. And when I find you—and I will— you and I will have ourselves a nice little... chat?

Yours truly,
Mark Q. Weston."

The mystery man didn't have a name, of course—how many does a devil go by? But Gina had no doubt who she was dealing with. In fact, she was more riled by his audacity than terrified at his threat. She answered him on the same sheet:

"*Good luck with that, you mud-sucking prick. I doubt you have what it takes to keep up with me, so the only place you and I will ever 'chat' is in your wet dreams. Enjoy your acid trip, Loser!*

Sincerely yours,
Ima Laughlin Mayasov."

She put the note back, hoping he'd see it. They were both lab rats now, trapped in a huge maze where their paths would likely cross. For Gina, though, it was a race against time. If she stayed ahead of the man who called himself Question Mark, she'd be safe. It all came down to strategy, endurance, and plain old luck.

But she couldn't plan ahead. A sharp crack—a breaking stick—sent chills up her spine. Was he near? She dove into a patch of shrubbery nearby, crouching low, eyes fixed on the trail. Footsteps followed—slow, deliberate, meant to conceal. Her heart pounded so hard she feared it would give her away. Deep breaths were dangerous. Stillness was her only refuge.

The cause of her alarm soon appeared. He was closing the gap. She prayed he'd pass her by, but his movements weren't those of a hunter covering ground—they were those of a tiger in the grass. Something had alerted him. He lingered there, a horseshoe's toss away. Then he lit a cigarette—so close the smoke nearly made Gina sneeze. His face was bruised and swollen, adding cruelty to an already sinister cast.

"Frogs and snails and puppy entrails," she thought to herself, alluding to the nursery rhyme.

Suddenly something caught the man's attention, and Gina's blood froze. As he drifted toward the shrubs where she hid, her mind raced. What desperate course of action remained? Was there any chance of slipping his grasp? To her immense relief, he passed without noticing her.

But horror surged anew when she saw him pull the note from the tree. Now he knew he was close—the ink was still fresh. He dropped his cigarette and crushed it under his boot, unwilling to betray himself with smoke. He scoped the area, searching for clues. Gina's dismay peaked when he stopped and stared directly at the foliage concealing her. A glint lit his eyes, a faint grin tugging at his mouth, and he began moving toward her with deliberate slowness. The last chapter of her life, she thought, was about to unfold.

Then something else stirred in the forest. A faint noise. A shift of weight. A presence. The man abruptly changed course, drawn off by the disturbance.

When he vanished from sight, Gina seized her chance. She slipped from hiding and limped down the trail in the opposite direction—her sprained ankle turning every step into a negotiation with pain. She pushed on anyway. Failure was not an option. She had to reach her vehicle. But with night falling, her chances were dimming.

Exhaustion eventually forced her to stop. She needed rest. Only a few minutes, she told herself—nothing more. She left the trail for cover and settled at the base of a tree ringed with bushes. She closed her eyes for what felt like a heartbeat. Yet when she opened them, darkness had swallowed the forest. Her sense of time had failed, and the realization magnified her fear.

She closed her eyes again, folding her hands in prayer, asking for deliverance. She longed for home—the familiar faces, warm meals, game shows humming in the background, dominoes and checkers and bingo with friends. All of it felt impossibly distant. More than anything, she wanted a bath. The odor surrounding her was wrong, unfamiliar, out of place.

She opened her eyes again.

Another pair stared into them.

She recognized them instantly—wild, unblinking, hungry. Her real ordeal had only just begun. One moment her nemesis was glaring at her, another and he was on top of her, tearing and clawing, sinking his teeth in her shoulder. The savagery was incomprehensible. She tried to fight him off, but was hardly his match. His strength was too great. Even the stench of his breath overpowered her. He immobilized her with ease, then positioned himself for the ultimate offense. Then pop. Exhausted, defeated, her world collapsing in on itself, Carly blanked. At least she would be spared the indignity.

In the ambulance, Gina surfaced briefly. Through the haze of shock and sedative, she made out the silhouettes of paramedics and the tubes in her arms. She was alive—surely a source of comfort. Shame, however, eclipsed pain. As tears gathering in her weary eyes, she managed to let out three trembling words before darkness reclaimed her.

"He violated me."

At the trail head, a sheriff and park ranger watched in silence as the ambulance disappear in a swirl of dust and leaves.

"Well," said the sheriff, "I got the scoop from the rescue team, but I'd like to hear it from the horse's mouth, as they say. What exactly happened here?"

"I was parked at the trail head," the ranger began. "Saw her heading in and had a bad feeling. Letting her go alone didn't sit right with me. Didn't want that on my conscience."

"So what'd you do?"

"Followed her, of course. She wasn't fast, but I was still on the radio when she suddenly upped and ran. Had to finish the call before going after her. By then she had a lead. When I finally caught up, she was standing by the pump station at Gorgy's Pass. She looked terrified. Told her who I was and offered to escort her back. Instead, she went for the ladder. I tried to stop her—too many pipes and cables up there. I had her by the ankle, but she kicked me—square in the face. Bam! Then she made like a fox and lost me in the woods. Took me twenty minutes to find her again. Glad I did. That was my Code One. When I radioed you."

"She have anything with her?" the sheriff probed.

"Just a backpack. Found this inside."

"Water bottle, notepad, red marker, thumbtacks... raunchy romance novel—*hmph!* That it?"

"Uh-huh. And this note on a tree. Take a look."

The sheriff read it, his frown softening to a faint, knowing smile.

"What do you make of it?" the ranger asked.

"Well, she ain't no mystery," the sheriff said. "Name's Gina Mae Wooledge. Seventy-eight. Dementia. Took off in a stolen vehicle this morning. Managed to drive herself up here somehow. Search didn't begin till the nursing home reported her absent. Poor lady... all those cuts and bruises. Cougar sure gave her a thrashin', dinnit."

"Yup. But she's safe now. Can't imagine what I'd have done if I hadn't found her in time. It was close."

"I'll say. Lucky your aim was good. She owes you her life, buddy. She'll have quite a story to tell when she gets back to the home, I'm sure. But you know what I think right now? I think you need to wind down. Been a long day."

The sheriff pulled a small pack from his shirt pocket.

"Care for a smoke?"

"No thanks," the ranger said with a tired smile. "Never smoked—and hell if I'm starting now."

Boccaccio's Boneyard

The Toadfish

The very deep did rot: O Christ!
That ever this should be!
Yea, slimy things did crawl with legs
Upon the slimy sea.

~ The Rime of the Ancient Mariner

A young man gagged at the sight of the odd thing dangling from his fishing rod. To look at it without revulsion required a level of grit he did not possess. His friend fared no better. The raw disgust rising in his gut escaped in a burst of profanity. "Holy shit! That's gotta be the ugliest motherf—whoa!—look out, dude! It's getting awfully pissed! Cut it loose!" The one holding the rod didn't hesitate. He flicked open his pocketknife, sliced the line, and the creature dropped back into the murky water, taking the hook, sinker, and brightly colored float. They had been fishing on the dock all day with nothing to show for it, and the grotesque thing they'd just released had ended their hopes with a final insult. It was getting late. There was nothing more to do but pack up and leave.

In the spot where the creature vanished, a column of brown bubbles rose to the surface and burst with a putrid stench.

The following day rolled without incident. The weather was mild, and by mid-afternoon the shoreline was an active scene. Nimble-footed sanderlings pattered along the surf. Gulls cackled and mewed overhead. A tall egret stood motionless in the cordgrass of a shallow tide pool, waiting for its next meal to drift by. Not far away, a ghost crab tugged at a mullet's carcass—until a dog barked, sending the crustacean scurrying into a hole.

Walking along the beach with her Jack Russell Terrier was an attractive thirty-something in casual summer attire. Her dog had found a dead mullet and was nosing it with curiosity.

"No, Rusty!" she called, waving him off. "Leave it!"

The dog bolted back to her, sneezing as he came, curiosity satisfied.

"You bonehead," she said with affectionate resignation, crouching to rub his face. "What should I do with you?"

"Osteocephalus," said a voice behind her in a warm Yorkshire accent.

She rose and turned to face a clean-cut man of similar age and good muscle tone.

"Excuse me?"

"Osteocephalus," he repeated, grinning. "Greek for 'bone-head.' Thought I'd be clever. Cheeky me. No offense to your dog."

"Uh-huh. And you're a sesquipedalian," she said dryly, not unfamiliar with the advances of would-be pretenders. "British?"

"That's right. Hope it's not a problem."

"Your opening line needs work," she said, eyeing him with cautious interest. "But I'll give you points for the word. Did you swallow a dictionary?"

"Not exactly. Borrowed it from a friend. He's a well-rounded bloke with a fetish for words."

"And that makes you...?"

"A friendly chap who enjoys meeting people," he said, extending his hand. "Ryan. Pleasure to meet you."

"Pleasure too, Mr. Friendly Chap," she replied, shaking his hand—still cautious but warming up to his good looks. "Carly."

"Pretty name."

"You can thank my parents."

"In more ways than one."

She raised a brow "Meaning?"

"Well, for one thing, they had you. Surely they deserve a medal. And their timing was impeccable. I could be talking to a dame or a little girl right now. Not a bad thing of itself, but..."

"Go on."

"The age wouldn't be right. I'm going out on a limb, but you're so beautiful I'd be mortified if the stork hadn't delivered you exactly when it did."

"That's... kind of sweet," Carly said, tucking a strand of hair behind her ear. "Careful. Compliments go straight to my head."

"And yet you allowed me to flatter you. I'm relieved. You could've brushed me off—or worse, I could be rubbing my jaw."

"No pain, no gain," Carly teased. "I can still connect one to your jaw if it helps."

"Thanks, I'm good," Ryan said with a smile.

Carly's armor cracked, and through the chink a smile emerged.

Sensing her softening, Ryan ventured: "There's a tiki hut with an open bar at my hotel. Right up the beach. Can I interest you in a drink?"

"Only if you're buying," Carly joked.

"I may have to," Ryan chuckled. "Open bar usually means mostly ice."

"Well, you certainly have no trouble breaking it. Lead the way?"

Something was growing between them as they went. Rusty, carefree as usual, trotted along. But a few minutes in, Carly paused. A small, brightly colored object bobbed in the waves, turning lazily in the tide. Her expression soured.

"People and their junk," she muttered. "I don't get it. When will they learn to put their trash where it belongs?"

"I hear you," Ryan said with a mischievous glint. "Thrift shops would be delighted. Some might even *wave* their listing fees —unless their hands are *tide* by excessive running costs. Do you *sea* what I'm saying? Either way, the beaches would be cleaner."

"You think?" Carly said, more amused by the attempt than annoyed by the puns.

"*Shore* they would."

Carly let out a reluctant laugh. "You're impossible."

The breeze smelled of Neptune's cologne—a briny thalassic tang, though slightly different today. Ignoring it, the twosome walked on, flirtation settling into something easy. Then Carly fell silent.

She found herself thinking about her job, and how people invest in each other the way they invest in the markets. Hedge-fund managers, all of us. Leveraging bets, hoping for gains, cutting losses when we must. Only hindsight tells us whether we chose well. Ryan felt like a worthwhile investment. A break from the tired patterns of her past.

She was still turning this over when they got to the tiki hut. Sliding onto a bar stool, she glanced at the man she was rapidly running out of reasons to doubt. A few seconds of sustained eye contact betrayed her growing warmth. Ryan met her gaze with a pleasant smile. Carly blushed.

Peeking over his shoulder, her lips then parted.

"Looks like we're the only ones here," she said softly.

"Oh, it'll fill up soon," Ryan assured her—still savoring the fine details of her cover-girl face when the moment was seized.

"Welcome to Cudas!" boomed the bartender: a dark, Johnny Cash clone whose upbeat manner contrasted oddly with his brooding appearance. "What can I get fer y'all?"

"For the lady..." Ryan began.

"Gin and tonic," Carly finished.

"And for me a Mojito.," Ryan said. Tall, double, on the rocks."

"Comin' right up," the bartender clipped, tipping his fiddler's cap.

Ryan beamed at Carly. "I'd be careful," he joked. "I had one of those in Thailand once and spent the whole night rocking like a boat. My mates still call me the HMS Ryan."

Carly laughed. "You're pathetic."

"True. Though the Thailand part is real. I was there two weeks ago."

"Oh? Doing what?"

"Playing sax at the Mandarin Oriental in Bangkok. I roam the globe. Hit up jazz clubs willing to book me."

"You're a musician! How fascinating. I love jazz. Smooth jazz, mostly. I even thought about taking sax lessons."

"Fancy that," Ryan said, tone dipping into something suggestive.

"I make an excellent sax partner. You like smooth; I'm more hard-bop. But anything works. When do we jam?"

Carly gave him a sidelong glance. "Just like that, huh?"

Ryan's eyebrows arched. "Only if you want. I'm not pushy."

"You're incorrigible," Carly scoffed, barely hiding the grin as she bent down to pet Rusty. "Beastly is the proper word."

Their drinks arrived with two ice-water chasers.

"Compliments of the house," the bartender said with a wink. Whether generosity or thrift, no one knew. They toasted anyway.

"Mmm! You've got to try this," Ryan said after sampling his highball.

"I'll pass," Carly said, squeezing a lime wedge. "Mojitos are cough medicine."

Ryan took another sip and winced. "Bollocks! Heavy on the rum."

He rinsed it down with his chaser.

Meanwhile, the bartender had drifted to the far corner, staring out at the ocean with a troubled expression. Carly and Ryan exchanged a look, then flagged him over. Just as he'd hoped.

Mooring himself like a oil tanker, he slapped his palms on the bar.

"No shrimp boats," he said. "No watercraft of any kind. Didja notice?"

Carly and Ryan shook their heads. "Can't say we did, Mister...?"

"Kroyer. And I s'pose ya didn't see all the fish washin' up. From Port Arthur to Brownsville, cordin' to the news."

"I might've seen one," Carly said. "What do you think it is?"

"Red tide," Kroyer grunted. "Algae bloom. Happens every few years. Even more now with all this global-warmin' crap they're talkin' 'bout. Bad fer shrimpin'. Bad fer water sports. Bad fer my cantina. Either of ya fish?"

"Not I," said Ryan.

"Neither do I," said Carly.

"Well, don't. Whatever ya catch'll be dead, dyin', or toxic. And ya sure as hell don't wanna eat it. I saw me a bad tarpon once. Looked like sumpin' the devil would keep in a fishbowl. Damn thing was all boogered up. Stank like sewer too. But y'all don't wanna hear that."

Carly gagged.

"And lemme tell ya sumpin'," Kroyer continued. "This tide'll bring up stuff that don't belong topside. Stuff from way down below. Best leave it be—if ya happen to come 'cross it."

"Thanks for the warning," Ryan said.

Carly sneered as Kroyer turned away.

"Seafood—not on my list anymore."

"Pity," Ryan said. "I was going to ask you to dinner. They're serving the geoduck special. Side of Rocky Mountain oysters.

"Oh, that's disgusting! You serious? No—of course you're not."

They laughed.

Suddenly, music filled the air. People gathered in the courtyard, drawn by the beats of a punchy Calypso band.

Ryan lit up.

"That's Yellow Bird!" he said, twisting his torso to the rhythm. "Come on—let's dance!"

They rose, leaving behind two empty glasses, a generous tip, and the cold stare of two rafter-mounted barracudas.

For the next couple of hours, they danced, laughed and wandered, letting the rhythms guide them. Later, they settled at a patio table, Rusty curled beneath. Their conversation drifted from movies to books to half-forgotten memories—the kind of easy talk that happens when two people begin to fall into step with each other.

The sun sagged toward the horizon, staining the sky with warm colors. A mild breeze swept in from the Gulf. The air felt heavier now, as if the sea were holding its breath.

When the moment felt right, Ryan leaned in and whispered something in Carly's ear. She was smitten. Her feelings had steadily grown, but now they surged. She rested her chin on one of her hands and laid the free one over his.

"Do you cry, Ryan?" she asked suddenly.

"What?"

"Do you ever cry?"

Ryan sniffed the salty air. "Never. Not the type."

"Come on. All men cry."

"Not this one."

"Be honest. What makes you cry?"

"Honestly, I don't," he said. "Cross my heart, hope to die. Someday. When I'm old."

"Ryan, please." He sighed.

"You're not giving up. Alright. But what then? Do I have to eat quiche?"

"I really want to know."

"Fine." He fumbled for a moment. "You know that song by Journey?"

"Which one?"

"Faithfully. I choke up every time I hear it."

Ryan leaned back, closing his eyes. "There. I've said it. My reputation—gone."

He said this in a humorous vein, but Carly sensed she'd reached a part of him no one else had.

"That's an interesting choice," she said. "I wouldn't have guessed."

Ryan's eyes welled slightly. Second-hand smoke from a nearby table.

"Not a choice," he said. "It's just what it is."

"So if you had someone to feel that way about, you would?"

"At the drop of a hat," he said, meeting her gaze.

Carly's body quivered, electrified by emotions and desires unfulfilled. The wheels in her mind spun like propellers, and soon the idea surfaced.

"You know what's funny, Ryan?" she said. "I think I left Rusty's leash in my bungalow. Will you walk me there? It isn't far from here."

Ryan gave her a knowing look. Moments later, they were back on the beach, following the path they'd taken before. Carly tucked her hand in the pocket of her shorts. The leash was going nowhere.

As they neared the bungalow, Carly spotted the brightly colored object she'd seen earlier in the waves—only now it bobbed in the surf. She stepped toward it, intent on retrieving it for proper disposal. Reaching into the water, she realized it wasn't just a float, but a fishing rig. Something heavy tugged at the other end of it, still submerged in the churning foam around her legs. She pulled on the line.

What happened next eludes comprehension. Something burst from the water and fastened itself to her leg. For a fleeting instant, there was no pain—only the blunt shock, the jolt, the sheer impossibility of what she was seeing: a bulbous, wart-covered mass with ungodly eyes and a mouth full of suture needles, wrenching and grinding at flesh and bone. And then the agony kicked in.

Carly's back arched as she fell to the sand screaming, a sound that tore through the beach. The pain was extreme, but she dared not touch the awful creature, fearing it would only make matters worse. Its body bristled with natural defenses—a living arsenal she could not navigate.

Rusty erupted into a frenzy, barking and snapping with fearless devotion. Ryan froze for a heartbeat, stunned by the surreal violence unfolding before him, then sprang into action. He grabbed the creature by its lightly protected tail and pulled with all his might, but the slick, narrow grip offered nothing. The thing held fast.

"Oh God!" Carly groaned, teeth clenched. "The pain! It's killing me! Get it off—please—get it off!"

Flustered and desperate, Ryan seized the fishing line dangling from the creature's mouth and yanked hard. Nothing.

Carly fought through the agony just enough to lift her wrist, around which a key-chain was looped. Her voice trembled. "Over there... please. Take me to my bungalow. I don't want to die in the sand."

"You're not going to die, Carly," Ryan said, voice taut but resolute. "I'll take you there. We'll take this thing off. I promise. Just hang in there."

He helped her to her feet, supporting her as she hobbled toward the bungalow. Rusty followed in her bloody footprints, whining and yelping.

Once inside, Ryan eased Carly onto the couch—upon which she immediately flew into panic.

"Easy, Carly!" Ryan shouted. "I'm calling an ambulance!"

"No! I want it off! Get it off now!"

"Okay—okay. Hold on. I've got an idea."

"Hurry! I can't take this any longer!"

Ryan tossed his phone aside and sprinted to the kitchen, tearing through drawers with frantic urgency. He returned with a knife, gripping it with trembling resolve. Driving the blade toward the creature, he hoped to land in a vulnerable spot—but when steel met hide, the thing reacted with a violent surge, bristling with a melange of cartilaginous quills, one of which harpooned Ryan's hand, causing him to drop the knife.

"Damn you, sonofabitch!" he shouted, clutching his gored fist.

Carly shrieked as the creature tightened, her voice cracking under the strain.

"Make it stop!"

Ryan bolted back into the kitchen and returned with a bottle he'd found beneath the sink. With extreme care to avoid Carly, he poured the caustic liquid over the creature. It instantly convulsed, releasing its grip and dropping to the floor, thrashing wildly as it tried to rid itself of the burning substance.

Ryan didn't hesitate. He lifted Carly from the couch and carried her to the bedroom, closing the door behind. For the moment, they were out of danger. He laid her on the bed, gathered some towels and returned with supplies from the bathroom. Carly moaned, gripping her leg above the wound, her breaths shallow and quivery. Seconds elapsed like a tortoise in a race race for its life.

"There," Ryan said at last. "The bleeding stopped. You're all patched up. This buys us time. I'm calling an ambulance now. Where's my phone?"

Carly's eyes widened suddenly. "Rusty!"

"Shit!" Ryan yelled. "My phone's in the living room."

Rusty's furious barking echoed through the bungalow, rising to a fevered crescendo. There were sounds of things tumbling and going to pieces. The noises grew more violent—grunts, growls, a scuffle, a frenzy—until a single, small whimper cut through the air. Then silence.

Carly shattered. "Ruuustyyyy!" she screamed, moving toward the door.

"No!" Ryan shouted as the hinges creaked. "Dammit, Carly, don't!"

Limping from the bedroom, she found herself in a war zone. An eerie stillness reigned over the scene. She stood amid the ruin, scoping the landscape for any movement. Then something stirred in a corner of the room. Painfully, she moved toward it, hoping to reunite with her beloved pet—only to freeze in her footsteps.

There, half-hidden in the wreckage, the creature lifted its head—its ghastly mouth flexing jubilantly.

Visible through the translucent skin of its distended belly, Carly saw something moving inside. Whatever it had consumed was still reacting to the powerful digestive processes at work—its outline shifting, twitching, growing weaker, fainter, until the only movement left was a swirl of gummy flesh in a cocktail of liquefied nutrients.

Carly collapsed. Seconds later, Ryan rushed in and froze, stunned by what he saw. The creature had nearly doubled its size, its swollen abdomen and bulging eyes augmenting its grotesque appearance. The stench it emitted only deepened the sense of wrongness.

Snatching a baseball bat Carly kept for emergencies, Ryan charged. He struck the creature again and again, but the blows landed with little effect, as though he were pounding a rubber tire. Still he continued, pushing himself to exhaustion before finally pausing for breath.

The moment he stopped, the creature seized its chance. With sudden, feral speed, it launched itself at him.

Ryan reacted instinctively, swinging wide and deflecting the airborne mass before it could reach him. The creature slammed into the wall, dropped to the floor, and lay still.

Cautiously, Ryan approached, hoping the impact had ended the threat. But then its goggle eyes snapped into motion, darting wildly around before fixing on him with predatory intent.

With renewed fury, it lunged—its long, curved teeth snapping toward him. Ryan struck its jaws, hoping to hinder its ability to engulf larger prey. He targeted its oddly shaped ventral and pectoral fins as well, the appendages that allowed it to swim, crawl, climb, and—he now knew—leap. The blows did little.

In a final, desperate move, Ryan drove the bat deep into the creature's gaping mouth. The beast recoiled, giving him precious few seconds while it struggled with the obstruction.

Wasting no time, Ryan took Carly in his arms and carried her outside. He still had her keys, which he used to open her car—a Roadster convertible parked nearby.

Strapping her securely in the passenger seat, he closed the door, dashed around, and jumped behind the wheel, where he noticed an accessory in the side pocket. Soon they were en route to the hospital.

Carly briefly regained consciousness, but seemed in a daze, mumbling incoherently about needles in her leg. Ryan was not overly worried. At least she was talking. The best part was they had gotten away. Ryan leaned back in his seat. All he needed now was to focus on getting Carly help.

On a lonely stretch of coastal highway, he pressed the accelerator. The Roadster's V8 engine roared to life, climbing past a hundred as the car surged forward. Ryan felt in control, knowing the worst was behind them. He even allowed himself a small, exhausted smile as he adjusted the rear-view mirror.

A devilish face sneered back at him.

Ryan slammed the brakes. The Roadster swerved and fishtailed, tires screeching as he fought the wheel. The sudden stop hurled the creature forward, sending it tumbling between the headrests and occupants—where it frantically snapped as it fought to regain its balance.

Ryan didn't hesitate. He reached for the automatic umbrella beside him and swung, striking the creature squarely.

Luck intervened. The creature's teeth clamped onto the umbrella's handle, triggering the release mechanism. Ryan hit the gas and retracted the convertible's power top. The roof pivoted upward and folded back, exposing the cabin to the rushing night air. The umbrella swelled, instantly pulling the creature from the vehicle.

The thing hit the asphalt hard, tumbling end over end in the Roadster's wake before coming to rest on the highway. Amid the battered remains of the umbrella, its misshapen head rose.

Darkness suited it; the night seemed to sharpen its senses. Like a rogue missile reacquiring its target, it fixed its bulbous eyes on the retreating taillights and began to track them keenly. But as the Roadster shrank in the distance, the creature noticed a new presence—a looming brightness growing behind it. It swung around, sneering at the oncoming glare, its jaws opening wide in a reckless display of challenge. The approaching vehicle did not slow. An instant later, the creature vanished beneath the massive tires of a semi-tractor-trailer. The impact was decisive, leaving nothing but a smudge behind as the truck thundered past and continued down the highway.

Sometime later, still driving along the nearly deserted road, Ryan noticed a troubling shift. Carly was no longer complaining. She had sunk into a heavy, unnatural lethargy.

With rising concern, he called out her name, reasoning that if she didn't answer, the cause might be serious. Envenomation. Septic shock. Something else. The possibilities mobbed his brain. If he didn't get her to the emergency room fast, she could slip into a coma—or worse.

So it was no small wonder when Carly broke silence.

"Stop!" she ordered.

"What? Carly, are you okay?"

"Stop, I say! Pull over the goddamn car!"

"What—why? You're going to the hospital. You need to see a doctor. Just a few more kilometers."

"Over there! That pullout by the dunes!"

Ryan flicked a quick glance at her—long enough to see the wild, glassy urgency in her eyes before snapping his attention back to the road. She was clearly unwell; he was certain of that. But then it dawned.

"Okay, I get it," he said, reasoning she needed to relieve herself or maybe throw up.

"I'm pulling over."

He rolled to a stop, shifted into park, set the emergency brake, and—with the engine still running—leaned back in his seat again.

By now the horizon had swallowed the sun; the crimson stains of its bloody feast fading slowly from the western sky. The moon, veiled in diaphanous clouds, cast a pallid glow that mingled with the shadows on the ground, producing a strange, twitching play in which sinister-looking plants seemed to dance macabrely on either side of the road. A squadron of brown pelicans—like the souls of ancient mariners—glid soundlessly over the marching waves, bound for destinations unknown.

"Here we are, Carly," Ryan said, almost afraid to disturb the air. "Anything I can do? Just name it."

Carly's gaze was fixed; her whole appearance, catatonic.

"Carly? Are you alright?" he asked.

No reply. No flicker of recognition. As though she were sealed inside herself, impervious to everything around her.

"Talk to me, Carly. Tell me what's wrong."

Ryan got his answer when her head turned and those strange, opalescent eyes—now bulging behind goggle-like corneas—locked onto his. A shudder ran through him as he realized Carly was changing before his eyes. Her skin rippled with rising knots and ridges, as though something beneath it were rearranging itself. Narrow slits opened along her neck, fluttering with a rhythmic pulse. Her jaw flexed unnaturally, and her teeth seemed to recede, replaced by several rows of needle-fine points pushing into place.

Ryan froze. Whatever was happening, it was too late to act. The air around him felt thin, numbing, as if draining his strength. Primitive instincts—alien, insistent—pressed in on his mind. They whispered of things hidden in the deep, of ancient remnants time had abandoned, of urges he could not understand and felt powerless to resist. In that haze, he understood what was expected of him as the creature that had once been Carly drew him closer, guiding him with its webbed appendages. Closer still, until his lips touched its cold, slick underside. There, a viscous secretion oozed from hidden glands, fastening him in place. His face twisted in pain, tears spilling as he tried to pull away, but his arms fell uselessly to his sides. Escape was no longer possible. He tried to cry out, but no sound came—only a strained, guttural noise rushing from his nostrils, which faded quickly as Ryan yielded to the role being forced upon him. His vision dimmed, his body seemed to contract, and the last traces of his self-awareness unraveled into nothing.

Police officers, responding to a report of an abandoned vehicle, arrived at the scene shortly thereafter. They found the Roadster with its headlights on and keys still in the ignition, but no sign of its occupants. The car showed no damage, no evidence of a struggle. On closer inspection, however, they noticed faint traces of an unusual residue leading away from the vehicle toward a narrow path between the dunes. Flashlights in hand, they followed the trail to a secluded stretch of beach. What they found there sent ripples up their spines: a single set of footprints leading toward the surf. Unusual footprints—wide, splayed, unmistakably webbed.

The officers could only watch as the incoming tide crept higher, wave by wave, erasing the prints two or three at a time. More waves rolled in, up the sandy slope in their timeless bid to resurface the beach, sweeping away the last of the impressions, until the sand lay smooth and unmarked beneath the moonlight.

Boccaccio's Boneyard

In the deepest parts of the ocean, few creatures survive without extraordinary adaptations. It is dark. It is cold. Food is scarce. Mates are extremely rare. But evolution has its own ingenuity. In certain species, the female, upon encountering the elusive male, draws him close. He attaches to her, fusing with her body, sustained by her blood. And there he remains for life—a ghoulish parasitic appendage, yet a vital organ.

A thrifty arrangement.

A reliable investment.

A most efficient tool for self-propagation in the darkest corners of the deep.

I Write, Therefore I Am

Nestled among younger buildings on the boulevard that shares its name stands one of the oldest churches in Paris. To the rapt admirer, Saint-Germain-des-Prés appears monolithic, impassive, untouched by the passage of time or the whims of urban fashion —though one might argue it quietly longs for the past, sharing little with what it deems its vain and obtrusive neighbors. The most conspicuous of these is Les Deux Magots: once a magnet for Apollinaire, Picasso, and Hemingway, now a mecca for tourists and the aspiring *corps d'élite*.

On one of my jaunts around the city, I discovered the popular café, and hastily made my way inside, lured by the promise of a savory éclair and multiple shots of coffee. This, however, a prelude to other enticements; for not long after—driven by an ever-nudging wanderlust—I parted the venue, and found myself draped in the shadow of the former abbey's imposing bell tower, whereupon I resolved to enter the church and discover what secrets lay hidden there.

Boccaccio's Boneyard

The ancient building yawned as I opened its massive twin doors—great jaws of wood they are—which nearly took my hand when they closed; a fair warning to anyone daring to intrude upon the slumbering giant. But intrude I did, and once inside found myself plunged in a gloom to which my eyes were not yet accustomed. Within these walls, light and shade exist, but our vision suffers most when abruptly stolen from either.

Despite the incommodity, I was able to ascertain, with very little doubt, that no other souls were present. This had a mesmeric effect on my imagination: a state in which I became witness to the trappings of another age—the dank atmosphere of the cloister; the heart-heavy echoes of the evensong; the mournful prayer of the pious recluse. And yet something was missing from the picture: that onerous weight of loneliness one expects when wandering unaccompanied in the hollow of a huge cavern, which, starved of light, this enclosure resembled. But that burden would be tolerated—even well received—if the alternative was less inviting.

Perhaps it was a test of my courage to abide in that place, for I soon felt the prickly sensation one gets when secretly being watched. I tried to shake it off, troubled by the unwelcome scrutiny, but it clung to me like a burdock. Inklings of this kind should never be dismissed, as ignoring them potentially invites danger. So I looked all around, straining for a glimpse of my hidden voyeur, but nothing in the dimly lit scene revealed the source of my apprehension. Real or not, my spy had eluded me.

Now, for a small tribute—mutely suggested by an unpretentious little coin box—one may purchase a candle, which can then be lit and reverently placed in a brass holder by the altar, as others have done who have not lingered. The wan light given off by this collective hommage, along with whatever the unthirsty windows are able to imbibe, provides the visitor the least illumination required to examine the interior when services are not underway. My candle found its place among the many assembled there, most of which burned brightly, imparting the air with a mystical scent and a mysterious, diaphanous haze. A few, however, had gone extinct, leaving little but a ring of melted wax —a testament to their impermanence. This gave me food for thought, but then my eyes adjusted to the dark and began to feast on their surroundings.

It is impossible to capture in a phrase the monumental awe this church inspires with its magnificent colonnades, fabulous triforiums, radiant clerestories, and empyrean vaults; or to confine to a sentence the overwhelming humility and sense of privilege one feels when loitering amid such grandeur. If the heart is a mallet and the pen a chisel, what can the poet aspire to carve? How can one mimic with words what the sculptor has eloquently wrought in stone?

Some will scoff at my appraisal of this monument, rambling on about how it is just another old church—worthy of admiration, but hardly deserving of such effusion as I have shown here; whereas I contend, with all due respect for those who dissent, that I have not given it half the acclaim it deserves.

There are, of course, many other churches in Paris; Notre-Dame being the most famous and arguably more colorful in architecture and history. I will not challenge the opinion, having toured the grand cathedral myself. But the church of Saint-Germain-des-Prés offers one thing all others lack—a distinction which, from a purely academic perspective, sets it boldly apart from the rest: René Descartes.

Here the great scholar found his final resting place. I was unaware of this when I first entered the church, and was surprised when I encountered his plaque—a moment of serendipity which, I confess, was the source of much exhilaration. And the reason was simple. Of the countless souls who have visited and will onward visit the master in repose, it was I to whom Fortune had gifted this particular moment of quiet survey, that I might pay my respects unhurried by others. A great honor, if three and a half centuries belated.

Lost in this reverie, I was suddenly distracted by a needling discomfort: the perception that I was now being observed more intently by unseen eyes. This time, however, I chose not to question its veracity or lack thereof—opting instead to focus my thoughts, ironically, on the man who questioned everything.

Here was a man who, along with Leibniz and Spinoza, began a revolution that shook the foundations of a continent mired in censorship. A man who gave us The Method: a germinal road map for many disciplines—physics, chemistry, astronomy, medicine— as well as metaphysics and epistemology. A man whose contributions to mathematics were cornerstones for Newton's own Principia Mathematica, ushering the world into a new era of discovery and invention without which many advancements would certainly have been delayed, if not forfeited. As an avowed rationalist, Descartes also reopened wounds in the short-sighted, which Xenophanes, Socrates, and Pyrrho had cut long before.

It is lamentable that Descartes's remains are enshrined in so modest a niche, tucked in a small chapel on the south side of a longish nave, squired by two monks with whom he had no acquaintance in life. Yet Descartes was a modest man. He almost certainly would not have balked at the arrangement.

How ironic, though, that a man whose books were banned by the Church; whose life's work contributed to its political decline; whose devout Catholic faith and pointed skepticism were alternately praised and reviled, was given this honor at all. Did this final act of inclusion represent, I wonder, the Church's twin proposal to offer and seek remission?

My thoughts were interrupted by what could only have been a cloud sailing overhead, for it seemed as though a great pall had descended over the church. Then a draft of air found its way inside—by which means I could not discern—for in that instant the candles were all snuffed out. A musty odor filled the air, the scent of the mausoleum. Then I heard rustling in the dark, and something brushed against my heel. Instinctively, I spun around to kick it in the blind, but nothing was there to suffer my punt. What was it that had touched me below the ankle? The sandal of a ghoulish penitent? The hem of a dead cleric's robe? The bony hand of a creeping corpse?

What would Descartes have done in that moment? What action would he have prescribed? How might I rightly conduct my reasoning so that I need not fret? All of these were questions perhaps better resolved in a café.

And yet, what if I had called upon the master? Could a soul take leave from *the undiscovere'd country from whose bourn no traveller returns?* If yes, what thoughts would he have tendered?

No, Descartes was dead. He could neither think nor be.

But though he shuffled off his mortal coil—his reason forever stilled—his soul yet breaths upon the parchment; his written word endures. Thus, in the immortality of his thought, he is.

Recent masonry work in the church had left a fine layer of dust on the gray mantle beside his tomb. When the light returned, I could see that the powdery film had remained undisturbed. Undisturbed, that is, but for a mouse's tiny tracks. Behold my spy and my phantom!, I crowed, admiring the stealthy rodent's written account of itself. It was then I realized that the source of many of our fears is often more trivial than perceived.

Suddenly, more tracks began to appear, only these were legible. Stroke by stroke, word for word, they spelled out a short, Latin phrase. I confess to a certain smugness watching it form, and smiled to myself upon its completion.

Scribo, Ergo Sum—I write, therefore I am.

Lingering in that mood where gravity and levity overlap, I fancied the author a mouse, a man, a master. Such things happen when light and shade commingle. Or, to vary the metaphor, when humility and hubris collide. And with that my mission—my road —was never more clear. It was time, I told myself, to quit the church; to leave the stale air behind. And as I turned around to plot my course, I reflected on my newfound confidence. It was good to think. Good to write. Good to be.

I could already smell the coffee.

Dead Men Don't Cry

"Let's see here. According to your file... you don't believe neutrinos exist?"

"No, I don't."

"Most scientists in the field do. "

"Right. And people once thought fire was a magical essence before we figured out combustion. Took a few heads rolling before folks started using theirs. When's my turn?"

"To use your head?"

"To lose it, Smart-ass."

"Why don't you think neutrinos exist?"

"Wolfgang Pauli."

"Help me out. I'm drawing a blank."

"Just messing with you, Bozo. The sine of the angle—squared. Stick that onto the kinetic part of the energy-momentum equation. You should see where I'm going."

"Energy is a vector? "

"*Momentum's* a vector. You knew that. But here's the real point: everything comes down to curvature. We're all just microbes stumbling around on a bent sheet of spacetime, thinking it's flat. Neutrinos? Pauli's ghost-particle band-aid for math he couldn't balance."

"But neutrinos have been detected in labs."

"No, they haven't. Lab nerds only think they have. They probably think fire is a magical essence too."

"Phlogiston."

"Yeah. That. Whatever."

"You also claim you don't believe in the Big Bang. Care to explain?"

"We live in a funhouse universe. Even you Oxford and Caltech geniuses admit spacetime is curved—but none of you follow that thought to its end. Galaxies settle into spacetime the way dew settles into the dimples of a golf ball. But when you look at them, you swear you're seeing redshift—galaxies racing away faster the farther they are. That's exactly what you'd see if you measure a curved surface with a straight ruler. Bend the ruler, and the "expansion" disappears. No Big Bang. Just mirrors in a funhouse. Look up the Pioneer Anomaly next time you're on the crapper. Same principle."

"What about entropy?"

"I need my phone."

"Not happening. What about entropy?"

"What about it?"

"All the hydrogen fusing into heavier elements? Heat bleeding away toward absolute zero? No energy left to do work? A one-way ticket to cosmic boredom."

"Really? Ever heard of black-hole jets? They're not just in-falling matter getting squeezed out. You're watching the birth of hydrogen—unthinkable amounts of it. Or maybe neutron streams going through beta decay. Either way, it's *recycled* matter being puked out by chubby black holes."

"Funny hearing all this from a trade school dropout and part-time chef. Not exactly your field."

"No—and a blind kid can't play basketball, a guy with no arms can't play guitar, and a double-leg amputee can't climb Everest—right? Tell that to Ben Underwood, Tony Melendez, and Mark Inglis. That's egg on your face. I need my phone. Or yours. Or a laptop. Anything with internet."

"And the antimatter? Where'd you get that? Since when does a guy like you have access to something like that? There isn't much antimatter in the universe to begin with. And producing it on Earth takes more than a schmuck—excuse me—a schmuck like you could ever dream of. No offense."

"Hah—ha—haaah!"

"Something amusing?"

"Thanks. I needed that. I find it hilarious that you think there's a cosmic imbalance—like Yahweh or Odin or Brahma forgot to flip his pancake. *"Ahhh! It's only cooked on one side!"* Quick: three seconds. How many sides does a Möbius strip have?"

"One."

"Bingo. One side, one edge. But show it to someone who's never seen one before. How many would *they* say it has?"

"Probably two."

"That's what I'm talking about. Scientists don't think in higher dimensions. Or if they do, they miss the big picture. Imagine two coins on a table, both heads up. Pretend one side is matter, the other antimatter. In three-dimensional space, gravity keeps them flat. But what if you manipulate the coin's orientation in higher-dimensional space. Flip one over and—kaboom!—your opposite-sided coins annihilate each other, along with the whole damn neighborhood. This is getting ridiculous. I really need a phone or a laptop."

"You found a way to flip the coin, didn't you."

"In higher-dimensional space, every particle, every pinball, every planet has two faces but one. A phone! Or a laptop with internet! Please!"

"What would you do if you had one?"

"Make your day."

"Hard to believe."

"You don't have a choice."

"You need to do better than that. The Lieutenant here would agree it's not wise to hand an ape a weapon."

"Is that what I am now? You flatter me."

"Not at all."

"From where I'm sitting, you're holding me to a higher standard. Come on, man—I need a connected device! It's important!"

"You're an intelligent guy. Why did you do it?"

"Blow up your pretty monument? Some people need their asses kicked before they'll listen."

"So what now—you're going to rub theirs?"

"The world's going down a shithole. You know it. Look around. Everything's a mess. People are out of their fuckin' minds. Politics, corruption, injustice—all of it. Everyone's got bats in their attic. I just wanted to shake people up. Make them do what's right. Clean up the Earth. Rescue the planet from the oligarchs. Make leaders pass an IQ test. Ditch our differences! Threaten the world if I had to."

"You look pale. Something wrong?"

"I need to do something soon. Please—give me a device."

"So you can pull another stunt like that? Not happening."

"You don't understand!"

"Let me lay it out, Brainiac. There's no chance in hell you're doing that again. You're going away for a long time. I'm not joking. They're locking you up tighter than a yellow brick at Fort Knox. And don't think your knowledge is a bargaining chip. I doubt you'd give up your secrets for free—but the Lieutenant here has friends who know how to get what they want."

"Believe me, they won't get their chance."

"You're sweating like a pig. Am I making you nervous?"

"I had a bad day. I wasn't thinking straight. My priorities were all over the place. So I built the damn thing. Did it for less than you'd pay for a box of Madeleine truffles. Yes, I blew up your famous monument, but then—"

"But then what?"

"But then I went one-eighty. When you brought me here. Something happened to me. I... I remembered this little girl I saw in the park the other day. She was with her mom. They were having fun blowing bubbles. A dog was chasing the bubbles and popping them. And the girl was laughing. Just laughing her little heart out, you know? Like nothing could ever go wrong in her world. Like she was happy in her own little bubble and it would stay that way. And then I thought about all of them—the kids, you know? Everywhere. They have their own little bubbles too. The world has to keep going for them. And I just... I only want to make things right."

"How will you do that?"

"There's another one."

"What? You mean—"

"I rigged..."

"Hey, that's a bad cough you have there. I think you need some help—Damn!—your face is redder than a beet! Lieutenant —get this man a doctor! Now!"

"I rigged... another... bomb. An iso... trop-ic... phase... invert... —a whole damn *barrelful* of coins!"

"What! You're kidding me! You've gotta be fuckin' kidding me! I don't believe you! Even you're not that insane! It's a goddamn bluff!"

"Yeah... sure, chief... a bluff. A pathetic... unconvincing... bluff. You had your chance... and you blew it... We could've... stopped..."

"What's wrong? What haven't you told me?"

"Cyanide... capsule. I took one... when I saw you coming. I wasn't... gonna give you my secrets."

"Shit! You said you'd changed your mind! You said you went one-eighty! Suppose you told the truth—what would you need a connected device for? Dammit, man! Answer me!"

"The count... down..."

"The countdown?"

"To stop... the... count—"

"FUCK!!"

Boccaccio's Boneyard

Knock Knock

The rain is pouring. The heavens are laden with grief. Gunmetal clouds—flashing, roaring, rumbling—salute the lost like massive, shapeless cannons. I could tell you a hundred stories, but none would be sorrier than Fabian's.

He was the fruit of a carefree, venturesome tryst between a young Brazilian college student and a mature woman of Scottish-Italian descent. For a while their passions ran deep, but the flames dwindled, and the lovers parted ways before the woman even suspected she had conceived. Fabian was born without a father.

Years passed, and Theo—the student—was now a successful and opulent businessman, happily married and raising a family that included twin teenage stepsons. His wife, Grace, was a woman of high rank and bearing, her skill at piano matched only by the ability to enrich the lives of her loved ones.

Theo often congratulated himself, believing he had acquired everything he had ever longed for and driven himself hard to achieve. But complacency is often rewarded with startling reversals, swift to remind us how small and powerless we are in the grand scheme of things.

One day, there was a knock on the front door of Theo's lofty estate. Answering it, he met a prim-looking man bearing a letter in hand and a boy at his side. The man introduced himself as the boy's temporary guardian, informing Theo that the mother had recently passed away—and, to Theo's surprise, that the boy was his hitherto unknown son. The letter confirmed it.

Fortunes of this caliber never turn without upheaval. At first, Fabian was apprehensive, but Theo—who until now had no natural children—was quick to welcome him. Grace, though taken aback, was kind and civil, not being lost on her husband's early dalliances or the knowledge that sowing wild oats can sometimes lead to a harvest. She took Fabian under her wing with the same genuine affection she had reserved for her own two sons.

This is not to say that Fabian's presence had no ill effect on the family's dynamics. The twins—Lucas and Bernard—feared the rift it would cause, and resentment took root. They teased the boy when Theo was away, and Fabian, in defending himself, sometimes worsened matters. Grace's patience grew thin, and she often lectured him.

Feeling isolated, Fabian retreated into a fantasy world where he, his father, and a dog he would name Beckett sailed the sunny South Pacific, island-hopping as far as Krakatau. He recorded these imaginary voyages on sheets of white paper with pencils, watercolors, and tears.

The hostility at home would soon find its echo at school. Some of his classmates—annoyed by what they perceived as favoritism—saw in Fabian the same thing Lucas and Bernard did: an interloper who excelled too easily. They bullied him, and when Theo questioned him about the bruises, Fabian confessed his regret for not playing the part of an "oaf," thinking it would have spared him the mistreatment. Theo gently admonished him, urging him never to think less of himself; promising too that he would speak to the school's administrators.

Thanks in part to the principal, a temporary reprieve was granted by his tormentors, and Fabian enjoyed a period of peace. He excelled in every subject and made a name for himself as a talented young artist, always drawing the same trio: his father, his dog, and himself.

Then, one day, he came home weak and without appetite. Grace offered to make him his favorite meal, but he declined and went to bed. After days of this, she finally examined him—and found bruises all over his body. When confronted, Fabian offered no explanation—noting he had not been mistreated. Theo did not disbelieve him, but the mystery gnawed at him.

Clinical tests later revealed the truth: hemolytic anemia, brought on by an extremely rare blood type, informally known as Golden Blood. Theo shared the trait, though he never showed symptoms.

Fabian required extensive treatment. The cruel irony of Golden Blood is that people who have it, though universal donors, can only receive transfusions from an equal. Theo was Fabian's only source. He didn't hesitate, of course. His love was boundless.

Fabian, however, had no wish to burden his father. Fighting back tears, Theo made him a promise: they were pals for life, and nothing—no illness, no expense, no individual—would ever come between them. Their bond was unbreakable.

Transfusions became frequent as Fabian's health declined. Theo gave what he could, which was insufficient; yet finding another donor was next to impossible. All the same, he did his best to lift the boy's spirits. One day, returning from one of his procedures, Fabian was greeted by an overly friendly year-old Vizsla. He embraced the dog immediately and named him Beckett. He then threw his arms around Theo, who held him tightly in return. Neither would forget.

Months rolled by in a rhythm of transfusions and short sea voyages aboard the bluewater sloop Theo had purchased. But they never ventured far—Fabian's treatments and Theo's business matters made long journeys impossible for the moment.

Grace pointed out the strain these activities were putting on the family, and tensions began to rise. Grace became combative.

Theo understood what was happening. He tried to reverse the damage and the growing friction with his wife and stepsons, but nothing seemed to mitigate their grievances.

Then came the alarming news: his business was failing. Revenues were plummeting and foreclosure loomed. He kept this from Grace, knowing what he risked if he told her the truth.

The pressures were growing. Theo struggled to keep them controlled, but how long he might was in doubt. And yet nothing could have prepared him for what came next. Fabian's troubles at school had resurfaced. Fabian was approached by a couple of bullies eager for entertainment. They twisted his words into an offense and began pushing him. Lucas and Bernard, standing nearby, rushed to his defense despite their differences. A scuffle erupted. A knife appeared. In seconds, two teenagers lay bleeding —one gravely injured, the other mortally wounded.

When Grace learned that Bernard was critically injured and Lucas had died, she went nearly berserk. Theo tried to console her, but instead became the target of recrimination, as it appeared to Grace that Fabian had instigated the fight. Even so, Theo prevailed upon her to endure the pain and rise above the calamity—for Bernard's sake and Fabian's.

Grace relented, but something inside her had broken already. She told Theo her feelings for him had dimmed and that she had contemplated divorce. A long discussion ensued, after which they agreed to live apart for a while, during which Theo would handle the business and Grace cleared her mind. A reunion was still possible. But when Theo learned that Grace was dating someone else, his hopes were shattered.

Bernard recovered. Fabian did not. His transfusions kept him afloat, but his underlying condition worsened. Doctors warned Theo that Fabian would soon weaken, lose mobility and speech, and eventually suffer organ failure. Transplants were his only hope —and even then, his odds were slim.

Theo's expenses were mounting. Fabian's treatments had cost him a fortune. Meanwhile, his lienholders were demanding payment. Desperate to avoid insolvency, he sold the equity in his house, most of his valuables, and even the sloop—the vessel he promised would take Fabian and Beckett to Krakatau.

Not long after, Fabian was admitted to the hospital. Beckett was allowed to stay by his side.

Boccaccio's Boneyard

Two weeks in, Fabian's condition plummeted. His liver and kidneys were failing. A donor was desperately needed, but none could be found. Theo's world was collapsing around him. His business was gone. His debts were mounting. His home, his wealth, his wife—gone. Now his son was dying. What else could go wrong. It was only a thought.

When Grace learned that Fabian was near death, she and Bernard rushed to the hospital. The mood they encountered was somber. Staff gathered outside the operating room, defeated. Beckett, held by an orderly, howled in the hallway, sensing loss.

The head surgeon approached Grace. A matching donor had been found at the last minute, he said. The operation proceeded, but Fabian did not respond well. He lived only a few hours. The surgeon handed Grace a picture the boy had drawn but not finished. A would-be gift for his father. A picture of a man, a dog, and a sailboat. A fuming island in the background. Many clouds. No sun.

Grace turned away. Something was in her eye.

What would Fabian have given to finish his picture.
What would I not have, to see that he did.

The rain is pouring. The sky is cloaked in sorrow. The rumbling clouds bring no solace to my grieving soul. Rest in peace, Fabian. I will mourn you now and forever—standing here alone, before your grave and mine.

Storytime

In a forest clearing on the fringes of nowhere, a group of young people sit around a campfire, idling away the night with songs and beer. The full moon plays at peekaboo through the clouds, illuminating and obscuring the landscape by turns. Jeff, Donovan, Keri, and Samantha are having a good time. Bob is silent and doesn't join in. After a lull in the revelry, Keri—a bit of a tart—suddenly pops an idea.

"Hey, guys," she says. "Let's tell some stories. The mood's right and there's no better place for it. So whaddaya think?"

Everyone but Bob nods.

"Yeah, why not?" they say.

"Why not," Keri echoes. "But we need some rules, and they go like this. First: the story has to be original. Second: it has to be creepy, scary, or shockingly good—no boring stuff made up on the spot. Third: not too long, not too short. Flash fiction is fine, but nothing we can hold our breath through. And fourth: no politics or divisive crap. It kills the vibe. Agreed?"

Boccaccio's Boneyard

"Agreed," they say—except Bob, who abstains from everything, including the beer Jeff gave him, though he still holds it tight.

Jeff takes the lead before Keri even finishes. He sees himself as the alpha mutt, though the others see him as plain old Jeff. After checking the rules with Keri again, he stands and begins.

Jeff's First Story —

"Alright, let's do this!" he says, rubbing his hands together. "So there was this guy once who ran into serious debt with some really bad hombres. The kind who'll take blood as an optional form of payment. Once you cross them, you're toast. Even if you pay late, you lose a hand or a foot—if you're lucky.

"So this guy skips town and hides out with his junkie girlfriend. She's supposed to keep him off the radar, but she snitches when she hears El Jefe has put a price on his head.

"El Jefe and his boys storm the hideout, drag the poor bastard into the woods, beat him senseless, and decapitate him. El Jefe has the body burned to ashes but keeps the head as a trophy—wants it stuffed and mounted like some wicked hunting prize. He hauls it back to his lair in a plastic bag and flings it into the closet where he keeps his weapons.

"Now get this: what the boss doesn't know is that a month earlier, the guy he knocked off—desperate for cash—volunteered for some weird research lab experiment. They inserted planarian genes into his DNA—planarians, those little flatworms that can regenerate from a tiny piece. You see where this is going." (Jeff doesn't mind spoiling the ending. He wants the early grins.)

"A couple days later, El Jefe and his boys are meeting in his lair, planning another hit, when the boss opens the closet door and—zoinks!—the debt-dodger is standing right there, machine guns at the ready. He's whole again! Grew all his parts back! So he mows down everyone in the room and walks away like nothing."

"No way, Jeff!" Keri says. "I'm not giving you a pass for that one."

"That was so stupid," Donovan adds, wiping beer from his nostrils. "How did he even—? Never mind."

Samantha rolls her eyes.

"I bet I can do better," Donovan says.

"Oh, you can?" Jeff shoots back. "Let's hear it then, homie. The floor is yours."

Donovan clears his throat, sits up straighter, and puts on a mock-serious face.

Donovan's First Story —

"So my story takes place in a courtroom," Donovan begins. "There's this guy on trial—the defendant."

"Like what else would he be?" Jeff mutters.

Donovan ignores him.

"The indictment lists hate-speech, hate-propaganda, racially-motivated harassment, conspiracy to undermine diversity, and sedition. The counsel claims he's unfit to stand trial by reason of insanity, but the guy waves him off, strides to the lectern like he owns the place, and starts addressing the judge directly.

"He declares himself of pure blood, insists racial hygiene is divinely mandated, sneers at laws protecting mixed unions, and scoffs at civil rights. Additionally, he rails against radical body alterations, calling them an abomination—a sin against Providence.

"People in the courtroom erupt. Protests, jeers, threats—the whole menagerie losing its collective mind. The accused snaps and launches himself at the crowd, a flailing cyclone of kicks and punches. Chaos spreads instantly: bodies shoving, wings flapping, claws scraping, fins slapping tile—a full-blown species-wide meltdown.

"The judge slams the gavel with one of his tentacles and bellows, 'Order in the court!' Then he gestures to the bailiff—a hulking brute with a gorilla's body and tortoise shell cranium—to restrain the defendant and haul him back to his cell as the court adjourns in pandemonium."

Donovan stops, pleased with himself.

"That's it?" Jeff asks. "That's the story?"

"You don't get it?" Donovan says. "It's a freak society. People go to cosmetic gene parlors to have their DNA edited any way they like. Pure human beings are misfits and outcasts in this society. They're being replaced by human-animal hybrids in a world dominated by franken-forms. GMOs are the new normal. Admit it. You loved it."

"I think I'm gonna barf," Jeff says.

"Don't you just love dystopian societies?" Keri says, voice flat as a dead battery—unimpressed.

"Maybe," Samantha says, mischievous.

Keri looks visibly disappointed. But now it's her turn. She clears her throat and begins with a brief introduction.

"Alright, fine—gather 'round. This one's quick but nasty."

The group falls silent.

"You've all heard the one about the woman who wanted to lose weight the quick and easy way, right? Diets never worked and she was terrified of scalpels, so what does she do? She swallows a pill with a tapeworm inside, and the thing goes fast at work, eating away the pounds. Sure, it's sick—but have you heard the one about the mango worm? And no, it's not something you get by eating the fruit."

The crickets chirp like they're waiting for the punchline.

"Alright," Keri says. "This won't be a long one, but I'll make it count."

Keri's First Story —

"So it begins with this glamorous girl—oh, about our age—whose dad happens to be a biologist, got that? He's just returned from a trip to Africa, where he led an expedition to collect samples of a certain insect's larvae. These larvae live in the ground—usually in mud—waiting for a mammal to wander by. When one does, they burrow into its skin and grow there until they're big and fat and ready to crawl out.

"Well, good ol' Dad brings home a petri dish full of these nasty little critters suspended in a paste—you know, so he can study them later. But his daughter knows nothing about it. So one night, after coming home from a night out with friends, she goes to take off her makeup. She's a little tipsy, sees the petri dish, and —because she's a genius—decides it must be cold cream. Rubs it all over her face. The next morning..."

"Stop!" Samantha cries, throwing up a hand, eyes tightly shut. "I don't want to hear it. Please."

Jeff is doubled over, wheezing; Donovan's laughing so hard he can barely breathe. It takes them a moment to wind down, their laughter tapering into little aftershocks.

Keri watches Samantha with a crooked smile. "Okay, okay—I get it. You're about to lose your lunch. I'll spare you... for now."

She flicks her hand.

"Go on, Sam. Your turn."

The fire pops softly as the boys catch their breath and all eyes shift to Samantha. She takes a moment, smoothing her hair, steadying herself. Soft-spoken as she is, she's still eager to add her link to the chain. After being politely asked to raise her voice a little, she begins to unravel her yarn.

"This is a story about broken promises."

Samantha's First Story —

"A woman is recovering in a hospital after giving birth. Emotionally she's a wreck—a bucket of tears—because her baby was born with a disfigurement the doctors could do nothing about. I'll spare the details, but let's just say his is a face only a mother could love.

"The room is dim. The only light is from a single lamp and the soft glow of the monitors. In the doorway stands a chaplain dressed all in gray. He doesn't announce himself. He doesn't step inside. He just stands there, like he's been there forever, listening.

The woman quietly prays, begging for an answer; asking the angels and saints what wrong she committed that her child should deserve such a fate. She even offers her life in exchange for his, which she's been told won't last long.

"The chaplain is moved by what he hears and finally speaks. After a brief introduction, he tells her he has the power to make things right—but only on one condition. She must take an oath. If he saves the boy and makes him well, she must keep it a secret for life. She must never reveal what happened, where it happened, or who made it happen. She must also understand that there is a reason for all things, even those she doesn't agree with, and that he and others like him are seldom allowed to change the course of destiny. No one is entitled to favors, and there is no free lunch.

"She agrees—but not before he warns her quietly and gravely that if she ever breaks her vow, the miracle will come undone.

"Years pass. Good and bad things happen to her, just as they do to everyone else. She accepts this wholeheartedly, remembering the chaplain's words. Yes, she had since lost her legs in a terrible accident, but she never forgot the blessing of survival—especially on this day.

"Her son, now a tall and handsome groom, is standing before the altar, waiting for his bride to walk up the aisle. His mother watches from her wheelchair, seated next to a dear old friend who is terminally ill, yet made the effort to attend the wedding.

"The ceremony begins and marches on happily. As it nears the end, the woman's friend turns to remind her how fortunate she is to have lived to see her son get married, wishing her the joyful prospect of grandchildren. The mother is deeply touched by this and tries to comfort her friend, who she knows will not live to see her own son marry.

"Then a thought hits her. She hesitates—knowing full well the line she's about to cross—pulling back again and again, as if each breath might save her from the mistake gathering at the edge of her tongue. But mercy gets the better of her. She leans in, unable to help herself, and whispers something into her friend's ear.

"A blood-curdling scream pierces the air.

"You see, just as the bride and groom were about to kiss, everything changed. But not all for the worse, mind you. As the bride reels back from the horror she's just witnessed, she sees her new mother-in-law running up to console her."

"Wow!" Jeff says, leading the applause.

"That was good, Sam!" Keri adds, clapping and whistling with the others.

"Bravo!" Donovan shouts. "Bravooo!"

Bob remains unimpressed.

Samantha gives a playful curtsy and sits back down.

Jeff's turn is up again, but his friends are skeptical now. After his first gag, they expect more horseplay.

"Ladies and gentlemen," he begins grandly. "We all came here for one thing alone. To have a great time. I shall spare no effort in the quest to achieve it. So without further ado, I bring you... drumroll, please... The Kachina!"

"Oh brother," Keri mutters.

"Damn! I knew it!" Donovan says. "Another doll story. It's another doll story, isn't it? He's gonna tell us another doll story. Like we need one more."

"I hate dolls," Samantha says. "They give me the creeps."

"It sounds like the Zuni fetish in that Karen Brown movie," Keri says.

"It's Black, peaches," Donovan corrects. "Karen Black."

"Whatever the name," Keri responds. "I couldn't care less. And quit calling me 'peaches'."

"Relax, all of you—will ya?" Jeff says. "I haven't even begun my story and you're shooting me down in flames. Hear me out."

"You had your chance," Keri says, looking bored. "Besides, who wants to hear about a stupid doll chasing down a lady with his spear?"

"Make it quick," Donovan says.

"Ah, but chasing down the ladies is what this is all about," Jeff tells Keri with a wink, "though not with his spear."

"I'm listening," Donovan says, cracking peanut shells and popping the treats into his mouth.

Samantha pretends to cover her ears.

"This better be good," Keri warns. "My impatience meter is going on tilt."

Jeff doesn't hesitate. He launches into his preamble.

"Alright, then. My next story is about this mysterious little dude you see in Southwestern rock art a lot. You've probably heard of him—the humpbacked flute player: Kokopelli. One of those kachina spirits in the Pueblo pantheon, so I've been told. Nobody really knows when he came on the scene. Some say a thousand years ago. Probably began as a guy with a pipe hauling a sack of goodies to trade with the locals, and the rock art is a Polaroid. But that's beside the point. You see, Kokopelli is often depicted in rock art with a phallus."

"Okay, this is getting interesting," Keri says.

"What's a phallus?" Samantha asks.

"A wiener," Keri explains.

"A tallywhacker, willie, sausage," Donovan adds.

"Ohhh...," Samantha says, stifling a nervous grin.

Jeff continues. "Yeah, but what does Kokopelli look like now? Wherever you see him today—on T-shirts, coffee mugs, lamp-shades, curtains—you'll notice he's missing something. Well, there's a story behind that, which is what I'm about to tell you. Ready?"

Jeff's Second Story —

"Martina was a broad who worked at a gift shop—and a pricey one at that. The job didn't pay much, but she and her husband Ramon, a mechanic, had to make ends meet, and two checks barely did it. Working long hours meant they hardly spent time together, and as you might guess, their eyes began to wander.

"Martina knew about Ramon's philandering but tried not to think about it. She'd pass the time daydreaming about things in the shop she couldn't afford. She was especially fascinated by a genuine Zuni—'scuse me, Hopi fetish there on display. An eighteen-inch-tall, anatomically correct Kokopelli doll carved from real cottonwood. Unfortunately, it was beyond her means. But anyone can wish, right?

"One day, a handsome rich guy walks into the shop: gold watch, fancy clothes, Black Card—the whole nine yards. He immediately takes a shine to Martina, who's very pretty, and it's not like she hates the attention. He notices she likes the doll and asks her if she wants it. She's stunned at first, but eventually accepts his offer.

"Pretty soon they're infatuated with each other and waste no time hopping in the sack. This goes on for weeks. Eventually, Ramon gets suspicious. One morning, over breakfast, he asks Martina where the expensive doll on the bedroom nightstand came from. She tells him she'd won it in a raffle organized by her manager.

"Ramon doesn't buy it. He secretly checks out her story at the gift shop, where one of Martina's coworkers accidentally spills the beans. Ramon is enraged, but remains quiet, planning to catch Martina and her lover in the act.

"One night, when Martina is home and Ramon pretends he's working late, the rich guy sneaks into the house. Martina and her beau are going at it with a will when Ramon quietly arrives and peeks into the bedroom. His suspicions are tragically confirmed, but he controls himself, letting them finish their business, unaware he'd come and left.

"The next day, Martina goes to work. During her break she tries repeatedly to reach her lover with texts and calls, but doesn't get a response. It's only when she gets home that evening and enters the bedroom that the reason her beau didn't answer becomes all too painfully clear.

"Standing next to the nightstand is Ramon, bloody knife in hand, wearing a devilish grin. On the nightstand is Martina's Kokopelli doll. It has a brand-new pecker—as real as a cock in a barnyard.

"The incident made the headlines, and ever since then, Kokopelli is gender-neutral."

"Wait-uh-meh-nut!" Donovan says. "When did this supposedly happen? I can't remember a time when Kokopelli *did* have a giggle stick—rock art aside."

"Oh, I'd say about nineteen-seventy-five, give or take," Jeff says.

"Aha!" Donovan crows. "You said Martina 'texted' her lover. Nobody was texting back then, you doofus! Yeah, doctors and lawyers had their pagers, but why would Martina carry one? Did the rich guy give it to her?"

Keri and Samantha are too busy trading embarrassed laughs to mind the slip-up.

"Okay, you got me," Jeff concedes. "But don't say it wasn't a good yarn."

"It was priceless, amigo. Full marks."

Jeff and Donovan fist-bump. Bob, however, still isn't laughing.

"Hey, Bob! Shape up!" Donovan calls. "Why don't you get with the group?"

"Leave him alone," Jeff whispers. "He's in a pissy mood."

"I can't say I blame him," Donovan says. "The guy measures fun in Scovilles. I kinda feel sorry for him. But I think I know what'll cheer him up. Hey, Bob—this one's for you!"

Donovan draws a deep breath.

"You've all heard about the Peeping Tom who snuck inside the tank in a ladies portaloo, right? The guy got hauled away in cuffs—lucky he didn't get more than he bargained for. Well, my story is about a similar case. Much less hazardous to the rascal's health... yet with far bigger consequences."

Donovan's Second Story —

"The guy in my story was up for a promotion at this company where he worked. As a mid-level executive, he was careful not to let his obsession leak out, because so much was on the line. Still, to get his naughty fix, he devised a way to install hidden cameras in the ladies' rooms throughout the office building.

"Having amassed a ton of material in a very short span, he removed all the cameras and carefully secured the compromising footage on a thumb drive—not the cloud, which might've blown his whole operation.

"So on the big day, he's preparing a presentation he's giving before the announcement of his promotion by upper management. Huge event. Even his wife and adult kids are in attendance—wouldn't miss it for the world. What nobody knows, and he least of all, is that the presentation thumb drive in his laptop had been swapped out for the incriminating one. An accident with devastating results.

"Standing at the lectern, facing the crowd, he clicks the run button. Seconds into his speech, he hears a collective gasp. People are covering their eyes or staring in horror, jaws hanging open. His own family bolts for the exit. Only when he turns around and sees what's playing on the enormous screen behind him does he realize his horrendous mistake.

"With his dirty little secret exposed, he panics—yanking out cables, tearing out thumb drives, smashing laptops and equipment—all while the buffered footage keeps rolling. He even claws at the projection, yelling pathetically that he has a promotion coming up, bawling like a kid as he falls to his knees.

"Before he's let go and the cops arrive, people see him pounding his head on his office desk—which, of course, is no longer his.

"The moral of the story? Don't mess with technology if you've got a little secret to hide."

Donovan gets a round of half-hearted claps before taking his seat. When the applause dies away, Keri steps forward.

"My next story is dark," she says. "And a very sad one, too. You may not like it, but here it goes anyway."

Keri's Second Story —

"Mortimer was a miserable old bastard who lived alone in a big two-story house surrounded by a Gothic Revival fence—because of course he did. There wasn't a single thing the geezer didn't hate: dogs, cats, birds, noisy cars, noisy planes, the weather, his neighbors—and especially the little cognitively disabled boy next door whose toys kept ending up in his precious yard.

"One day, after a heavy winter snow, the boy came out to play and built himself a snowman. And not a cute one, either—this thing looked like a crime scene with a carrot. Empty eye sockets, a single wrecking-bar arm, the works. But the boy adored it, and honestly, it adored him back. He spent hours with it, since none of the other kids on the block would play with him.

"On Christmas Eve the weather warmed up. The boy came out in just a sweater, carrying a foam-rubber ball—the snowman's favorite, since it bounced off its icy body in every direction and made the boy laugh. But later that day, right as he was called in for dinner, the ball sailed over the fence and landed in Mortimer's yard, where it stayed until evening.

"Now, whenever Mortimer found a toy in his yard, his routine was to pick it up, swear like a sailor, and chuck it in the trash—where the boy sometimes managed to rescue it later. But this time 'Ebenezer' didn't notice the ball until he spotted the boy in his yard from a second-story window. Figuring the kid had come through the front gate to retrieve it, the heartless old coot decided to pull a prank to 'teach him a lesson.'

"He used his remote device to lock the gate, knowing the boy would have to climb the fence to get out. And because he was exactly the kind of man who shouldn't be allowed near children, he didn't bother to check whether the boy made it. He just went about his evening while the kid tried to escape.

"That night, in the middle of an untimely blizzard, Mortimer was awakened by the sound of an ambulance and someone wailing outside. He looked out the window and saw a man holding a distraught woman while paramedics worked to free the boy from the fence, where he'd gotten stuck. He'd frozen to death.

"Mortimer grinned. Problem solved. He celebrated with a cup of tea by the fireplace.

"Later that night, as he dozed in his armchair, he kept getting this prickly feeling that someone was trying to get into his house. But every time he checked, nothing was there. Eventually, lulled by the fire, he fell asleep.

"On Christmas morning, the police arrived in force, alerted by neighbors who'd heard strange noises and screams coming from the house. After forcing the fence open, they made their way to the front door, which they opened with the help of a locksmith.

"Inside, they found a lovely holiday tableau: an elderly man lying in a big pool of water, skull crushed. The only thing out of place was the presumed murder weapon—a wrecking bar lying on the floor next to the fireplace."

Keri leans back to a round of applause.

"That sure was dark," Donovan says. "Good one, Keri."

"Ditto," Jeff adds. "Mortimer was a real jerk. I felt for that little boy."

"Did you?" Samantha asks.

Everyone stares at each other. A burning log pops and crackles, sending up a thin column of ash that twirls in the air and disappears. An uneasy silence falls upon the circle. Jeff glances at Donovan; Keri straightens a little.

"Your stories were very well told," Samantha says. "I don't know if my next one will sing, but I'll give it a try."

She smooths out her skirt and folds her hands on her lap. The campfire dims a little and Samantha's features darken a bit. She pauses and thinks.

"Hmm... let's see. Okay—this one might suit."

Samantha's Second Story —

"Once upon a time there were four high school friends. A couple of boys and a couple of girls. They wanted to check out this old, forgotten cemetery deep in the woods where there used to be a town, long before it was abandoned due to a mine fire.

"They all piled into a Jeep and drove for an hour on rocky roads to where they wanted to go. When they got there, they set up camp. They were having a good time, but after a while got bored and decided to do something wild and crazy.

"One of the boys had an idea—a bad one. He thought it would be cool to break into one of the tombs and pull out a body, which they did, even though one of the girls thought it wasn't right. They pulled out the mummy of a twelve-year-old boy and propped him up by the campfire. They put beer in his hand, just like he was one of the group. They even called him Bob, which probably wasn't his real name since the inscription had weathered away. And then they began telling stories..."

"Hey, wait—that's our story," Jeff says. "It doesn't count."

"C'mon, Jeff, give her a break," Donovan says.

"No, Jeff's right," Keri breaks in. "Rule two, subsection two: no boring stuff made up on the spot. We all agreed."

"Well, there you have it," Donovan says. "Her story didn't meet the criteria for exclusion. The rule states—and I quote it —'No boring stuff made up on the spot.' I don't think Sam's tale is boring at all. What do you think?"

"Will you guys let me finish?" Samantha flares—her soft nature barely aggravated.

Keri and the guys fall sheepishly quiet. After a moment of mild tension, Samantha continues.

"So Bob has no reason to shape up and get with the group. He's been asleep for a hundred years and these clowns wake him up in the most unfashionable and disrespectful way. If anything, he *is* pissed. So the moment they least expect, he stirs to life and gives them a chase. They all freak out and run for their lives, learning their lesson the hard way. The end."

An awkward stillness fills the air. Samantha looks around, but no one looks back. They sit there, nursing their wounds.

"We get it, Sam," Keri says. "It was a bad call. A wrong move. We know it. But don't come down so hard. Jeff and Don will put him back now, right guys? And not just throw him back—give the guy the respect he deserves."

"Like they haven't done that already," Samantha mumbles.

Jeff and Don return the corpse to its tomb. They don't say much while they do it. The broken slab they pried loose earlier lies at an awkward angle, and the boys have to wrestle it back into place. The joke has curdled, and the night feels cooler than before.

When the last scrape of stone settles, they step away in silence. They put out the campfire and switch on their flashlights, preparing to call it a night. They're just about ready to go to their tents when Keri lets out a gasp.

The moon still plays its game of peekaboo in the clouds, and when the cemetery was briefly bathed in its light, Keri saw something move.

"Guys! Did you see that?" Keri says in a hushed, strangled voice.

"Huh? See what?" Jeff asks.

"You didn't see it?" she repeats, keeping her voice low. "One of the statues over there—the one behind those headstones. It moved. I swear it did!"

Jeff, Donovan, and Samantha swing their flashlights around.

"Come on, Keri," Donovan says. "We know you're all worked up by the one about Bob, but you need to let it go."

"No, really!" Keri insists. "I'm telling you what I saw. That statue there moved. First it was looking that way, now it's looking at us."

"Right," Jeff says. "The boneyard is haunted and the spooks are coming out. Let's run."

"Don't patronize me," Keri snaps, slapping his arm.

"I dunno," Jeff says. "Your marble friend looks normal to me. If you call that normal."

"I want to go home," Samantha says. "Let's get out of here." The moon ducks behind the clouds, and darkness drops over them like a curtain. The trees around them whisper in the breeze. The last ember in the campfire sizzles and expires in its bed of wet ashes.

Then the flashlights go out. All of them.

"Okay, now that's hairy," Donovan says. "What the heck just happened? All of them at once? You gotta be kidding."

"Shhh!" Keri hisses. "Did you hear that?"

"Yeah, I heard it," Jeff says. "Everyone quiet."

"Over there—where Keri pointed," Donovan whispers.

"No—more to the right," Jeff says.

"Guyyys..." Samantha says, voice trembling. "I think someone's behind us."

"I think two," Keri says. "Oh, this is bad. Really bad. They're getting closer, guys. Do something!"

Jeff lets out a terrible howl—then silence.

"Jeff!" Donovan shouts, fumbling blindly in the dark. A moment later, a heavy thud shakes the ground.

"Don?" Keri calls out. "Are you okay?—Jeff? Are you there? Talk to me."

An eternity compresses into a few seconds. Something shuffles in the dark. The moon refuses to help. Samantha trembles.

"Mommyyyy…" she whispers. She doesn't move. She doesn't dare. The faces of her friends crowd her mind, pounding at her temples. Then—a noise.

"Who's there?" she whispers. "Keri? Say something."

Someone approaches. Heavy footsteps. No doubt.

"Don?" Samantha whispers. "Is that you? Oh, thank God. I was afraid you were hurt. Over here—follow my voice. Reach out and grab my hand. There. Don't let go. Let's not get separated.

"Now, if only I can find my lighter. I think it's in my bag. I'm pretty sure it's this way. Careful, Don, don't trip. We're almost there.

"….Why is your hand so cold?"

Boccaccio's Boneyard

The Hippie House

On the southwest corner of 169th and Schneider, in the city of Hammond, there used to be—not far from the house where I lived—another which no longer impinges on the scene.

As kids, we called it the Hippie House, because of the inveterate reputation it had acquired, deservedly or not, as being a sanctuary—prior to its conclusive abandonment—to that bohemian class of dissidents after whom it was christened.

By the time I had the courage to peek inside, the two-story dwelling was in a ramshackle state, having partially survived an arson attempt, which rendered it structurally unsound and off limits to hippies, hobos, and kids—fearless and foolish—who found rapture in exploring its creaky hallways and gutted rooms.

The year was nineteen-seventy, if memory serves me right, when its carcass of half-charred walls and rafters was finally torn down by order of the City Council. All that was left was a ring of oak trees hemming its loamy footprint, which gave the property the appearance of a miniature forest with a hollow in its heart.

The property remained vacant for a time, overgrown with grass and weeds, despite being marked as the future site of an overflow parking lot for the clinic across the street—now an annex to Purdue University Northwest Campus. It ultimately fulfilled that role, but I still picture a house where only asphalt prevails.

I had the sad privilege of knowing the boy who had last lived in that house. Sad, because I am privy to a certain knowledge I wish I could disclaim. His name eludes me today, but I still remember him as a likable, if somewhat crestfallen playmate who shared with me an abiding interest in dinosaurs, earth-moving toys, and model spacecraft. A Johnny-Come-Lately who did not stick around long enough to lose the moniker.

"Johnny" and I were only friends for a few weeks. Scarcely had his family moved in when the house was abruptly abandoned; the mystery surrounding their sudden departure forever remaining unsolved. The father was probably that hard-working head of household who was always searching for greener pastures, every choice of habitation merely a leg in the route toward stability. One may never know.

I never met the stern patriarch, but stern he was, according to his son—a fact for which I needed no convincing, given the occasion I heard the man yelling at him from the shadows of an open door, commanding him to the table. A rattling experience, which echoes to this day in the darkest halls of my recollection. Something in my gut would shrink whenever Johnny was hailed.

The source of my concern was a braided bullwhip hung high on the wall behind the door I mentioned, which I once caught a glimpse of as my friend was called in. When I later asked him about it, he told me, with shocking indifference, that his father would sometimes use it on him. O, the grim revelation. Yet the strangest part is that Johnny never complained—not to me or anyone else. I have always wondered if he was coached into silent submission.

There was always apprehension in Johnny's movements whenever his father cried out for him. On one occasion, while answering a particularly harsh summons, he dropped his Major Matt Mason action figure in the sand pit behind his house, where we often played. I found the toy astronaut buried there months after the family had left. Its arms and legs had gone limp, the way Johnny's would at the sound of his father's voice. But Johnny seldom displayed emotion.

I returned the major to his grave.

Now, the grist of my story lies not in what might have occurred in that house while it was occupied by Johnny's family, but rather in the events that followed its abandonment, its subsequent occupation by squatters, and its ultimate destruction—events which suggest it had a long and dark history.

I have heard people say that they hear ghostly sounds in the parking lot just before dawn: saws cutting boards and hammers tapping nails, followed by alarming cries and howls of dismay—alluding, perhaps, to an accident which ended badly.

Then there are those who claim that on certain balmy nights one can detect, every now and then, the faint smell of weed or scented punk sticks. Others have assured me that if one perks up an ear in a warm summer breeze when all is peaceful and the traffic nonexistent, the distant pipes of Hendricks, Joplin, and Morrison can be heard, emanating from the twilight limits and the outer zone. Rumor has it that a local self-styled guru popped one too many reds while soaking up the vinyl vibes of his three favorite warblers, joining them promptly in the afterlife. His revenant is a rare but amusing spectacle, they say. Still others profess to have witnessed black-light imagery in the velvet clouds of an approaching storm while standing on the spot where the house was torched.

Then there are those who trod upon the site in the hours after sunset. They swear to have heard the muffled cries of a newborn babe who is nowhere to be seen. Detractors laugh at this, offering rational explanations for the otherwise uncanny phenomenon, such as a cat in heat mewing creepily in the shadows. On the other hand, one cannot dismiss the legend of a teenager girl who was noted as putting on a little weight, quitting school abruptly, and making herself scarce until a few months later when she enrolled again, slimmer. She and her family were very tight-lipped about the whole situation, offering dull excuses as to why the girl's stepdad later got life in the cooler.

Children who were, and then were not, is a tale twice told in this neighborhood. A girl nine autumns old would never see the colors of her tenth, yet the trees along the railroad east of Lindberg whisper their nightly hymns in her memory. She plays on the railroad tracks in moonlight, I am told, at a game of chicken.

Many haunting stories have been told and retold by the locals, giving rise to the perception that this vicinity on the outskirts of Chicago is... well, haunted. But who can say. One is left wondering whether any or all of it is real as told, or simple misrepresentations of mundane origin.

But of all the stories and anecdotes I have heard, one in particular strikes a familiar note. Some people have perceived, in the languorous hours between dusk and dawn, the ethereal sound of lashes. One... two... three... four... Sometimes it goes on. All without a whimper of protest.

Yet no one, as far as I am aware, has ever seen a boy of eight or nine standing alone in the parking lot, deep in the night. The welts on his arms and legs are conspicuous. But if you ever do, and you try to approach him, and he does not take flight, he just might ask you if you have seen his toy astronaut—the kind made of plastisol with a wire skeleton that easily breaks. Damage which does not register on its face.

You know where to find it.

Boccaccio's Boneyard

U-47

U-47, the pride of Hitler's Kriegsmarine, surfaced like a saltwater crocodile rising from the murk. Smoke unfurled from the exhaust ports as the twin diesel engines rumbled awake, feeding power into the hungry batteries deep within the hull. Cold brine streamed off the plating in sheets, taking with it the stale breath of unseen depths. Then a hatch clanged open, and Kapitänleutnant Günther Schreiber stepped onto the conning tower's wintergarten. He inhaled the night air with a proprietary satisfaction, as though the ocean itself had been waiting for him.

Night was always the best time to rise. Cloaked in darkness, the U-boat became a rumor—a shape the enemy might sense but never see. Under this cover, Schreiber could stalk his targets with little concern for the forty-four men sealed inside the steel coffin with him. Four torpedoes sat primed in their tubes, and he felt the familiar itch to give the order.

The waters between the zero and thirtieth north parallels of the western Atlantic were prime hunting grounds—a vast, indifferent wilderness where navy ships, merchant vessels, and especially the lumbering tankers drifted into the crosshairs of men like him. Schreiber knew they were out there. He could almost smell the oil, the sweat, the human fear. It was only a matter of time before one wandered into his trap.

He had chalked up many kills, but the thrill never dulled. Each attack felt like the first: a baptism of fire, blood, and exultation. He had consigned countless souls to the deep, yet his appetite remained sharp. If the opportunity presented itself—and it would—he would seize it without hesitation. Like a wolf scenting blood, he scanned the horizon for prey. Tonight, fortune favored him.

He was fine-tuning his field glasses when the sea finally offered him a gift. A shape. A silhouette. A promise.

"Kontakt!" he barked, the word bursting from him like a shot from a deck gun.

He turned to his first officer, eyes bright with predatory joy. *"Auf geht's."*

They descended the ladder and sealed the hatch behind them. With its batteries charged and ballast tanks flooded, the leviathan dipped beneath the waves, sliding into the dark with the grace of something born there.

U-47 was on a mission of ominous weight, and Schreiber felt destiny coiling around him like a familiar appendage. The target loomed in the periscope—massive, inert, a bone begging to be cracked.

Schreiber's teeth chattered with anticipation as the crosshairs settled. When the range was perfect, he gave the command:

"Los eins! ... Los zwei! ... Los drei! ... Los vier!"

"Im Wasser!" his first officer confirmed. Now there was nothing to do but wait.

For a heartbeat, there was only silence—a death-like stillness—before the world tore open.

A fiery mushroom blossomed in the periscope. A moment later, the concussion slammed into the U-boat, rattling bolts and ribs alike. But she held steady. She always did.

Above, chaos reigned. Chairs and bodies were flung like toys. Steel buckled. Flames roared through corridors. Men who had been laughing in the galley an hour earlier now clawed through smoke, searching for comrades, for exits, for miracles. Some tried to rescue the injured, stumbling through heat so intense it warped their vision. Irony hung over them like a pall—they had been discussing maritime tragedies earlier, unaware that their own chapter was being written.

Schreiber ordered the ballast tanks blown. U-47 rose again, breaching the surface like a revenant. He wanted his crew to witness the spectacle—the inferno, the ruin, the proof of their efficiency. And he knew they were safe. At this distance, illuminated by the oil-fed firestorm, there would be no reprisal.

The destruction was absolute. Yet as he watched, something inside him shifted. A faint tremor passed through him—not from cold, nor from the engines, but from some small, mutinous part of himself he could no longer silence. The sight did not satisfy.

The exhilaration of the kill—the old thrill of snapping an enemy's spine—had thinned to a thread.

Time after time he had pursued targets with ravenous expectation, only to find the reward hollow. And now, staring into the burning remains, he understood what he had always known: none of this was for him. Not for his glory, nor for the men who followed him with blind loyalty. They were all bound by duty to a man who saw them as expendable—rags to be discarded once his boots were polished.

They, too, were victims.

If Schreiber had any tears left, he might have shed one.

Somewhere on the high seas, he had found his humanity— and there it would remain, unreachable, forever.

Decades pass. Wars end. Flags change. The ocean remains impassive, unfeeling, detached. Beneath it lie the scattered relics of other ages: guns, anchors, broken hulls. And now, in one corner of its restless expanse, a new fire burned upon the waves.

Eleven men died in the explosion. One hundred and fifteen more abandoned the inferno in lifeboats, drifting far from the devastation. Maydays crackled into the night. All they could do now was wait.

But confusion spread among the survivors. A rescue boat was apparently missing. Several swore they had seen it, yet none could explain its disappearance. Had it been called away? Had it fled? Was it the same vessel glimpsed earlier in a fog bank? One injured man, sedated and half-delirious, claimed he had seen skeletons— stark, jointed shapes swaying in the firelight. Perhaps metal framework. Perhaps morphine. Perhaps something else.

Some laughed. Others prayed.

In time, help would arrive, and those who lived were pulled from the sea.

Months later, investigators determined the cause of the accident. Failure in a high-pressure system. Methane gas had escaped in tremendous volume and ignited. A preventable disaster, perhaps, but difficult to predict. Such conclusions offer little comfort, only the certainty that it will happen again.

The offshore platform *Deepwater Horizon* was the latest name on a long list of postwar maritime disasters, joining the Kirk Pride and SS El Faro, taken by storms; and the Atlantic Empress and Burmah Agate, shattered in collisions. Men would call the blast an industrial failure. Yet the sea cares little for such distinctions. To the deep, all wreckage is kin—whether born of torpedoes, tempest, or negligence.

And so the pattern continues.

No one knows where the next tragedy will strike. One can only hope to avert it, pray it never comes, or—failing that—offer a moment of silence for those claimed by the sea. The kingdom of the deep embraces them all.

Captain Schreiber and his crew still stand at attention on the upper deck of U-47, deep in its ocean trench. There, the *Flying Deutschmann*—enrobed in rusticles and marine life—keeps its final, eternal watch.

Boccaccio's Boneyard

Vanity

A long time ago, I heard a funny story. An old wives' tale, one might call it—or, more precisely, a young bachelorettes' tale. The zany little yarn, as I remember it, went something like this: If, on Halloween, a young woman stares long enough in the mirror while eating an apple and brushing her hair, she will see her true love gazing back at her—or so the rumor claimed.

Let us ignore, for the moment, what qualifies as "long enough," and forget the sheer terror such an apparition would likely provoke in our youthful subject, even if she were expecting it. The real question is what the image in the mirror actually represents. My first impression was that it foretold the nymph's future boyfriend, husband, or lover. But with a few of life's lessons under my belt, I've come to believe the tale is far wittier than I once thought, and that "her true love" was actually a reference to the conjuring maiden's real object of interest, considering the amount of time she spent before the glass: herself. I don't know what part the apple plays in all of this, but given that it seldom accompanies a woman who is grooming herself, I suspect it serves as a decoy, meant to distract us from the otherwise narcissistic nature of the ritual.

Here's where the funny ends.

Now, for the main course.

A good friend of mine, Thomas J. Warner, was a gym instructor. The "J" stood for Juggernaut. That's right—don't ask me what his parents were smoking. He never expanded on the initial and I never pried. I unraveled it by accident one day when he left his driver's license in my truck, which he had borrowed. When I returned it, he gave me an icy look—and let me tell you: it was wise not to smirk.

TJ got into bodybuilding in his early teens and developed a powerful physique. Later, he traded barbells for books and earned himself a business degree. He worked at a brokerage firm right out of college, then put in sixty-hour weeks at a major advertising agency. But the circean call of physical fitness proved irresistible. He ditched the tie, bought a run-down gym, cleaned it up, renovated it, and eventually launched a chain of popular workout venues all throughout the region—success he credited to his schooling and experience. It also made him massively rich.

Now, TJ was a mite big for his boots, and—as one might suspect—he let his wealth go to his head. One day, while sampling our stouts at a local bar and grill, he told me about a life-sized painting of himself he'd commissioned for the main lobby of his flagship gym. He was a popinjay, of course—likable, if arrogant— forever working to burnish his public image. But this latest craze truly took the cake. Listening to him rave about it was like enduring a... well, never mind. He spent the rest of our meeting crooning over that two-dimensional centerpiece of manic obsession—paraphilia might be the better word. In need of an anesthetic, I ordered myself another brew.

Yes, TJ was proud of what he'd accomplished in a such a short span—and rightly so. He was smart, ambitious, opportunistic, and these traits carried him far. But he also craved attention; not that I would ever soil his memory. Still, it was evident to me—and to anyone who knew him—that he constantly required heavy doses of praise and adulation from the people around him; not quite reaching the height of demand, but exasperating enough for those not given to fawning, myself included.

One time he showed up at my place in a mint 1958 T-Bird—something he'd always wanted to add to his harem, which included a two-tone Bugatti Veyron, a black Lamborghini Murciélago, and a classic 1969 Corvette Stingray in gold, previously owned, he claimed, by some jet-setting corporate tycoon whose name I thankfully forget. He bragged about it the way a soccer mom gushes over her kid winning the Junior World Cup. He even made me take a dozen stills of him posing with it.

Besides the fast and flashy cars, TJ had an eye for the ladies— and they for him. I had my squeeze, and she was my only. But my Casanova buddy had many—each paraded like a prize-winning heifer at a county livestock show, the sum of their collective jewelry nearly matching his own. Those were the days.

I can still see him sauntering down the sidewalk with that comical swagger of his; flexing for admirers at the gym; blowing kisses at fans from his Veyron; tipping waiters with wads of cash. Each gesture delivered with the careless charm of a man convinced the world adored him—moments I'd gladly call back if such things were possible.

But in the spring of last year, something changed about him. He began to lose interest in that one singular focus of his devotion: his portrait. It appeared to have lost its cult status, and I couldn't gather why. Creases formed on TJ's forehead when I asked him how it held up under the attentions of "countless throngs" lining up to admire it. He wasn't amused. But he did confide something I'd never expected to hear: he didn't want it anymore. He asked if I would accept it as a gift.

"Thanks," I told him, "but one object of devotion is good enough for me."

Several days passed with no contact between us. Then, one evening, he called. He sounded as though something had scared the bejesus out of him. He wouldn't say what, despite my attempts to extract it. Instead, he begged me to come to the gym right away. I agreed, though I warned him I'd be an hour. I could hear the spike of anxiety in his voice when I told him he'd have to wait—odd, coming from a man I'd always considered my unofficial bodyguard whenever our drives took us through the hoods.

When I finally arrived, TJ was pacing outside, visibly shaken. I had never seen such a wide-eyed look on his face. He was genuinely terrified. I asked him what the trouble was, but he only gestured frantically for me to follow, whimpering now and then like a newborn pup searching for its mother.

Inside, without daring to look, he pointed toward the portrait. He still hadn't spoken a word. While I examined the thing, he hovered by the door, as if ready to bolt at the slightest provocation. He kept his head down the entire time, refusing even a glance at his likeness, though I saw nothing amiss. I struggled to understand the problem, and an equal struggle arose as I tried to decide how much of this circus was his doing. I warned him he was making fools of us both, but he seized my arm and dragged me outside, trying to explain himself through a jumble of mangled phrases and erratic hand signals.

This went on for several minutes. Annoyed by this behavior and having had enough, I grabbed him by the placket of his shirt and demanded he pull himself together. He managed to steady his breathing, and when he finally found his voice, I could hardly believe what came out—the ramblings of a child waking from a nightmare.

He told me everyone had gone home for the night, and he was about to lock up when it happened. He'd paused to admire his portrait—a routine act of reverence, no doubt—and laid his hand upon it. At that moment, he said, the image stirred to life —a grotesque mockery of himself—and grabbed him by the wrist, sneering wickedly as it tried to pull him in. But he managed to wrench himself free and flee the building.

He said that in the weeks leading up to the incident, he'd noticed small changes in the portrait—subtle movements caught through the corner of his eye; something he'd chalked up to fatigue. He also claimed it whispered to him when he was alone. Not words, exactly. More like garbled noises: hisses and groans welling up from an unseen depth.

I wasn't buying it. I figured he'd taken something he shouldn't have, though he insisted he was clean—and to his credit, nothing about him contradicted his claim. Besides, it was hard for me to imagine a man who prized health and fitness above everything—save his ego—dabbling in something that might tarnish his brain.

Even so, he begged me. He wanted the portrait gone—burned, if possible. His was a bizarre request, but I told him I'd handle it—in the morning. He thanked me with a kind of strained relief, the urgency beneath his voice unmistakable.

We left the gym and headed to our usual hangout. After a long talk, I managed to convince him that his "doppelganger" was nothing more than a trick of his mind—an illusion, a fever dream, the sort of thing everyone experiences at least once or twice in life. My explanation seemed to settle him. His shoulders loosened, his breathing relaxed, and he even found his appetite again, tearing into a plate of buffalo wings.

Bit by bit, he came back to himself, thanking me for helping him through what he called a bout of "mental flatulence." I told him not to mention it.

When we finished our stouts, I offered to drive him back to the gym where his T-Bird was parked. He nodded, we paid, and out we went. On the road, we agreed—at length—that the whole episode should be boxed and shelved, never to be revisited. We even laughed about it. By the time I dropped him off, he was noticeably in better spirits. I gave him a thumbs-up; he returned it. Then I pulled away, thinking the night's madness had finally run its course.

I was puzzled, though, when he failed to show up at the gym the following day. It was closed, of course, but we'd agreed I would dispose of the portrait, and I needed to know whether the plan

still stood. I assumed he'd simply forgotten; but unless he came, I had no way inside. Even more baffling was his silence. He didn't answer my calls. So after several days and twice as many attempts, I filed a missing-person report.

With the authorities' help, I got a locksmith to open the gym. Two officers followed me in, sweeping the place before giving the all clear. Everything was in order, yet there was no sign of TJ anywhere. His absence became even more perplexing when his car was found out back. Nothing in the cabin. The trunk empty. No clues. No trail.

It's been a year now and I'm still at a loss. TJ must have run afoul of something or I would have heard from him by now. I keep searching for answers to his abrupt and mysterious disappearance, checking in with the police from time to time in the hope that some lead might surface. It may take months, or years, but until that day comes, I'm still on the fence with regard to his request.

And while I'm on the subject, I did take down that vile portrait of his, just as he'd asked. But destroy it? I couldn't. I removed it from the gym—yes—and brought it to my house, where it now sits in the attic beneath a tarp, waiting in silence. Waiting for me to decide what to do.

Who knows. Maybe someday I'll haul it down and finish the job—get it over with, once and for all. I just haven't gotten myself to do it, wondering if it's the right thing. But I'll say *this* much: I'm still floored by how much trouble it was to get the blasted thing up there. It was so damned heavy.

Dark Matters

Kitty's my twin. Her real name is Katherine. We're not exactly alike, but you'd never know.

One day she did something weird. She told Mom that Grandpa had come to visit her—he'd died the month before. Mom didn't like the sound of that. I saw the worried look on her face. She didn't believe it, but the thought that Kitty was going crazy frightened her. Maybe Grandpa's death hit Kitty hard. Maybe it was messing up her mind. Maybe—Mom hoped—it would pass.

But Kitty kept on. She told Mom that Grandpa had promised her a pink rose, and that one had bloomed outside her bedroom window. Mom wasn't totally shocked; she'd planted the bush herself. But she freaked out when Kitty said Grandpa had told her he'd bring back her dead puppy. That hit Mom like a train. She'd never told Kitty the truth. She'd killed the pet by accident backing up her car, then lied about its absence—told Kitty the pup had wandered off with its animal friends. Later that night, Mom woke to an awful smell. Following her nose, she went to Kitty's bedroom. She peeked inside and almost hit the floor. Kitty was sitting up in bed, cradling the pup in her arms. It was rotten. She looked up at Mom, smiled, and put a finger to her lips.

When Dad got home from his trip, Mom pretended nothing was wrong. She'd cleaned everything up and given Kitty a bath. Kitty was now asleep. But Mom couldn't hide her feelings. Dad knew something was wrong by the way she looked. When he finally got her to talk, he was shocked, heartbroken, angry. He didn't say it then, but we knew his thoughts. Grandpa was never good for Kitty. He was a fly in the pudding. Dad was glad he was gone.

Kitty was always good with puzzles. Not jigsaw puzzles—well, yes, those too. But most of all word puzzles, word games, wordplay. It was a hobby she and Grandpa shared. They'd play a lot together. He'd taught her many things: finding patterns, using ciphers, breaking codes. He'd say stuff like "Never odd or even" or "Was it a cat I saw?" and she'd repeat him, word for word. Or she'd say something like "Dormitory," and he'd spring back chuckling —"Dirty Room!" Other times they'd talk gibberish. These were Kitty's favorite pastimes. Grandpa encouraged her, and often spoiled her with gifts not meant to be parted with. Sometimes he whispered things not to be shared. That's why Kitty adored him so.

No one cried more when he died.

Not long after, Kitty found a book in a closet. It had belonged to Grandpa. It was old and smelled like basement. It was full of strange writing and pictures no one understood or knew the purpose of. But Kitty did. She knew.

She opened it slowly and began to read. Her heart was pounding. This wasn't some boring schoolbook. It felt like holding a box of lightning. Like something about to go boom! She felt naughty holding it—and she knew why.

She had found something forbidden.

As she turned the pages, the lights in the room flickered, things tinkled or shifted slightly around her, the shadows in the room began to dance. The air tasted like thunderstorm.

Kitty continued to read—her eyes flaring like a spring-loaded cat as she gobbled every word and picture; her appetite growing with each passing moment. Strange symbols, stars and spirals, people dancing in circles, and writing—wormlike scribbles and flourishes; letters that looked like prayers turned backward. Her breath deepened. The hair on the back of her neck rose. The more she read, the more she felt the energy, the power.

Her lips peeled back in a crooked grin—as if she'd been blind all her life, then suddenly shown the universe and all of its secrets. It was wonderful. It was magical. It was like... giving up the ghost.

Soon she discovered she could do things she'd never imagined. Like finding hidden objects not meant to be found. Like knowing events before they happened. Like moving things around without touching them.

Like pulling things from the other side.

Mom was making our bed one day when Kitty began to slip. That's when the show began—when Kitty told Mom about Grandpa and the rose he'd promised her. When she dug up her dead puppy. Mom and Dad knew they had a problem. At first it didn't seem like much; a thing that would probably fix itself over time and with proper healing. Then, one night, they heard Kitty talking in her bed. I should know—I was there. Mom kept a canary in a cage. Kitty, half awake, said it would "fly out the window," and "Beware the hawk!" I know it sounds mean, but it was kind of fun to watch. Then Kitty fell asleep, and so did I. Mom and Dad were still at the door, listening from behind.

Mom was very upset the next morning. She'd been cleaning the birdcage when her canary got out. It flew across the room, out the window, and onto a tree branch in the yard. She hoped it would fly back.

Then the hawk hit—and then it was gone. A few yellow feathers floated softly to the ground. Dad was amazed by this. Coincidences happen, he thought, and this was one of those times. Mom wasn't so sure. She started to pray again.

Another time, Dad was in his shop, working with some tools. I brought him a tray of cookies I'd made for him, when a wing nut flew off the counter-top and landed on it. Dad was all mixed up, wondering how it'd done that. I thought it was pretty cool. It was fun watching him scratch his head while he looked the tray, the wing nut, and the tool in his hand.

One day, Kitty and I were playing with our dolls. Mom popped in the bedroom with some fresh linens. She was changing the bed sheet when looked at me. She paused for a moment, dropped what she was doing, and came to where I was sitting. She stared at me closely—told me she hadn't noticed my eyes before. Said they had a different shade. That made me uncomfortable. I told her to stop. She'd never told Kitty that. Mom kissed me on the forehead and went to finish her chores.

Then, one night, when the wind was howling, Mom was getting ready for bed. She was about to tuck herself in when she saw a shadow slip past her door. She thought her eyes were playing tricks, so she went to investigate.

Dad—in bed with a stomach ache—shot upright when Mom started screaming. It took him a while to calm her down, and when she finally spoke, she told him what she'd seen. Grandpa was back, she said. Inside the house. Standing at the end of the hallway, looking at her. His face was gray and yellow and sunken in places. He was holding a pink rose. She felt a cold draft and smelled soil.

Dad told her to get a grip. He went to the hallway himself, but saw nothing there. No ghost, no goblin, no Grandpa. Nowhere in the house. It was just a dream, he said. I think Mom wet herself. I couldn't stop giggling.

Dad was a bit gruff at the table the next morning.

"So, Kitty," he said, "about last night." His voice had a tone. "What was so funny that made you giggle?"

I'm glad he didn't look my way. Kitty had nothing to say. She rarely did, anymore.

Later that week, things got worse. Kitty became a problem at school—snapping at teachers, picking fights on the playground. It got really bad when she stabbed a classmate with her pencil. I wanted to help, but she was sent to the office. The principal told Dad not to bring her back.

At home, Mom and Dad fought. With everything going on, they started shouting and breaking things, blaming each other for all sorts of nonsense. Dad almost hit Mom. That would've been a sight. But before things fell apart, they made up.

Boccaccio's Boneyard

Kitty was still a problem, so they decided to try something different. The kind of thing where doctors take blood, then take see-through pictures of you, then ask a lot of questions and whisper to each other in private. But the doctors found nothing wrong—nothing to blame Kitty's behavior on—so they just gave her a shot. They didn't know what else to do. She got very quiet after that. Mom and Dad were told to keep an eye on her, lock her in her bedroom, and feed her pills for a while.

And wouldn't you know it: just like that, the problem ended. Kitty became as meek and docile as a lamb. No locks, no pills, no nothing. The house grew quiet again.

I watched and waited.

Dad said Kitty's illness had passed; that she'd gotten over Grandpa. Mom said it was prayer. Whatever it was, our family had found peace again—peace and serenity in a world of simple pleasures. A happy family of three, once more.

Kitty sleeps.
And only I know where.

You might think things are different with Kitty gone, but you'd be wrong. You see, *I'm* Kitty. We're not exactly alike, but you'd never know. I've learned the value of discretion, subtlety, stealth—the price of acceptance. There's still so much to see in this world; so much to experience. I think the possibilities are endless, fascinating, and thrilling beyond measure. The time will come soon enough.

Gramercy, "Grandfather." Thy misdeeds bear wondrous fruit.

Ah, and one more thing. Nothing metaphysical. But seen from the family's perspective—is not a bird in hand worth two in the bush?

Mom and Dad are calling.

I am coming.

I think I am going to like it here.

Boccaccio's Boneyard

The 13th Story

Or The Space Between Floors

"That which does not kill us makes us stronger."

Isn't that the tail wagging the dog? With apologies to Nietzsche, I believe the reverse holds true—at least in equal measure.

Consider this: countless things are given to strengthen, heal, or elevate a person, yet when they are resisted or rejected, the result is ruin—sometimes literal, sometimes figurative. The principle cuts both ways, whether we care to admit it or not.

Let's use the coronavirus as a Nietzschean example. It'll set the stage for what comes later.

The virus has one mission: replicate. It finds a host, hijacks its machinery, and turns it into a zombie confetti-popper—each confetto a tiny projectile seeking another host to continue the cycle. If you catch the bug and survive, you might be stronger for it. Nietzsche was right. And if you catch it and *don't* survive, he's right again. But every proposition has a flip-side, hence my suggestion: that some things destroy people through lack of it, not exposure to it. Let me explain.

A few years ago, I joined a cult.

Funny how that sounds, isn't it? What does Merriam-Webster say? *"A cult is a group, often with religious or ideological themes, characterized by excessive devotion to a person, idea, or objective, and frequently utilizing coercive, manipulative, or harmful practices to control its members. They are generally marked by intense dedication, isolation from society, and rigid, authoritarian leadership."*

I know what you're thinking: the weak link in the definition is "harmful practices," because what is harmful? Anyone up for debate? That's the trouble with language. It's ambiguous. It opens the floodgates to arguments and counter-arguments. But when you see the forest for the trees—the definition as a whole—well... that's for you to decide.

Anyway, I joined this cult, as I said. And wouldn't you know it? I'd found my happy spot—the one thing I'd always wanted. Everyone accepted me. No questions asked. I belonged instantly. And the best part was that I had a voice. My words mattered, all within the tight little framework of what was considered appropriate. True, the rules and etiquette were fastidious, as they are in any fandom or coterie, but I stayed well within the acceptable limits.

"Acceptable." It rolls off the tongue like a sweet caramel.

Worship was an absolute gas—and I don't mean that flippantly. Turns out I was a leader at heart. I often led the devotionals, and the congregation was so impressed by what I had to say that I was soon elevated to the sacrosanct office of Minister of the Congregation—master of ceremonies, if you will.

That was merely a springboard. I became the spiritual guide of our missionary vanguard, teaching persuasive methods of recruitment and techniques for easing the unfounded suspicions of prospective members. I enjoyed the work, especially breathing my personal afflatus upon the youth—a perfect sounding board for what the elders called charisma. Youth is a force to be reckoned with. Everything was going well.

Then it happened.

Word reached me that an auditor's investigation had uncovered sloppy record-keeping and accounting discrepancies involving a senior member. His documentation didn't distinguish church expenditures from personal charges. Rumor had it he flew first class, bought luxury cars and jewelry for himself and his girlfriend, and lavished expensive gifts on friends.

I questioned him privately. He showed no remorse, nor did he admit to anything. I told him it was fine—not to sweat it—and that if he'd done a disservice to the community, it was probably because his compensation was grossly inadequate, and his service to the congregation merited rewards far beyond his paycheck.

He thanked me with a smile, but not before leaning in to say he hoped never to have such an awkward moment with me again. I saw no reason for it.

Soon after, I noticed a hushed reverence developing around me. Natural, I suppose. I never expected to become the center of gravity around which the congregation orbited, but there I was. I was going viral. I just have a way of penetrating the human soul that is, quite frankly, phenomenal. I give people exactly what their spirits crave: inner tranquility. And the way they listen—eagerly, like someone savoring a ripe fruit—is the best testimonial I could ask for.

I'm their conscience, they say—a title I accept, not out of ego, but because it's true. My sermons are their compass. People hunger for direction, and I'm willing to point the way. Who else will they listen to? No one. I'm the architect of their peace, the navigator of their justification. It takes a rare brilliance to hold someone's entire world in your hands and reshape it. And why not? Greatness must recognize itself.

Not long after counseling the elder, one of our female congregants approached me. She was coy at first, but with gentle reassurances I coaxed her out of her shell. What she told me wasn't unheard of. She revealed she was in a partnership with a "celibate" man—though she herself was not.

I inquired further as to the nature of this partnership. She confessed to an affair. She was very distraught, for the man was a priest, and she remembered teachings from the elders that would have put her in a very bad position if her amorous nature were exposed—made worse by her choice of partner.

She wept, and my heart sank. I reassured her that what she was doing wasn't sinful in itself; humans have needs. It becomes a sin when people engage in a simulated act of procreation frivolously —that is, without respect for the blessed act of conception. As for the priest? A good disciple—and a bountiful wellspring of spiritual infusion. He was an excellent source for its delivery— something she would greatly benefit from.

She left with renewed determination.

Some time later, a well-tailored man—also a congregant—came before the council of elders to petition for the highest office in the congregation, claiming it as his divine right. Whispers of arrogance and shady dealings threatened to disqualify him. The council said his character didn't align with their mission.

I disagreed. He was a fighter—exactly what the congregation needed. Someone who knew how the world actually worked, not just someone who quoted scripture. A man whose past shouldn't interfere with his powerful future.

The council was still murmuring among themselves when I stepped in. By the time I finished, their objections had melted like wax near a flame. They elected him unanimously; not the least because it equally benefited them in ways I made clear.

Needless to say, my influence grew. People became more pleased with themselves, more forgiving of their own lapses, more adept at smoothing over their shame with a coat of self-satisfaction.

There were other times I made my mark. At the scene of a horrible but preventable accident—tragic, devastating, something that should have shattered them irreparably. But I whispered a reason, a divine purpose, a cosmic plan, which they clung to like a life raft.

When pandemics came, I offered them an explanation: punishment for the people they disliked. They nodded without hesitation, relieved to be spared the burden of introspection.

As for the slow erosion of modesty, courtesy, restraint, honor— those old-world relics—well, I helped them see such things for what they truly are: weaknesses, hindrances, outdated virtues that interfere with what matters most: the individual—that sacred island in a sea of self-absorbed, equally competitive souls. Once they understood that, everything became easier. For them and for me.

People are given a choice of paths; I merely offer the ones they already desire. You see, their moral compass is the one which points exactly where they've already decided to walk. You may judge them if you wish. It changes nothing. They will always walk the walk. *Their* walk.

And so we've come full circle. That which does not make people stronger—because they resist or reject it—often destroys them. And what often destroys them is what they reached for willingly, eagerly, with both hands.

I simply make the reaching easier.

Some call me indulgence. Some call me hubris. Some call me self-anesthetizing-delusion—SAD. But you know me best in that small, delicious moment when you see the tasty fruit that hides the worm and lean toward it.

I am always there.

And I always will be.

Boccaccio's Boneyard

AFTERWORD

When Hernán Cortés burned his ships in 1519—well, scuttled them—he did so to keep his mutinous men from slipping back to Spanish-held territory. With no way home, they were forced to commit fully to the conquest of the Aztec Empire. I chose this seamark event as an analogy for the effort I put into publishing this book. Writing it was the fun part. Preparing it for launch was something else entirely. Smoothing transitions, tightening prose, checking punctuation, minding syntax, and tending to a hundred other small but essential concerns became a daunting task—even with the benign assistance of an as-if human editor. It had to be perfect, at least in my own eyes. Without that standard, I might have tossed the whole thing aside, relegating it to the bucket list of projects forever stuck in queue. I might never have seen it published. I had to commit.

The solution was simple: assign an ISBN to the unpublished manuscript using the next number in a block of pre-purchased identifiers, then immediately apply for a Library of Congress Control Number. That act alone ensured I felt the pressure to finish what I had started. The LoC's patience has its limits.

It worked. Proof is in your hands.

In hindsight, there is not much I would change—not that I could, for that matter. Beyond cultivating interests, doing research, building vocabulary, and writing, the road to publishing is not especially steep. It is simply littered with wads of chewing gum, as it were.

But here it is: the book itself. With few exceptions, nothing gratifies me more than stepping back and looking at the nest from which I once dared to leap, the wandering path that brought me here, and the early promise of leaving behind a form of entertainment that readers may enjoy long after I'm gone. I have no trophies or medals to hand out, but to those who found pleasure in these stories, the pleasure was mine.

If you've made it this far, then you've walked with me through every shadow, every joke, every whisper, and every odd turn these stories offered. That alone makes the years of drafting and redrafting worthwhile. I wrote this book to leave something behind—something that might outlast me, or at least keep someone company on a quiet night. And now that it's in your hands, I feel the simple, unmistakable satisfaction of having followed through. I'm glad I burned the ships.

Will I write more? Of course!—granted the time. The creative impulse is still pumping strong, and I sense no weakening in the urge to shape new tales. I already have several half-molded stories lined up for the next anthology: not quite ready for the kiln, but definitely taking form. I even have a title in mind. I hope the finished product will be worthy of your interest and approval.

Finishing this book has reminded me why I write in the first place: to share that glow of imagination with anyone willing to meet me halfway. If these stories offered even a moment of escape, reflection, or amusement, then the long hours behind them were well spent. I'm grateful for every reader who takes this bold and exciting journey with me, and I look forward to the next one already taking shape.

ACKNOWLEDGMENTS

This book would not have come into being without the guidance, encouragement, and quiet generosity of those who shaped my creative life. I owe a debt to the teachers who first recognized my potential, to the colleagues who affirmed it, and to the many authors—living and long departed—whose works illuminated the path for me. I am grateful to the friends and readers who offered their time, their candor, and their patience as these stories took form. Their insights strengthened the work in ways they may never fully realize. Most of all, I thank my family. My children, whose gentle nudges kept me moving forward, and my wife, whose unwavering faith sustained me throughout its development—this book is as much yours as it is mine.

I am also grateful to Microsoft's Copilot, whose editorial partnership helped me refine this anthology with clarity and precision. Its assistance was instrumental in "tightening the screws" and preparing the manuscript for publication, all while respecting the inspirational bedrock and creative architecture of my work.

And to ChatGPT of OpenAI, for the haunting illustrations found in these pages. Their stark forms and unsettling textures lend the book an added layer of dread—an atmosphere that lingers like a shadow just beyond the edge of the text.

RECOMMENDED READS

Boccaccio, Giovanni. *The Decameron*. Penguin Classics, 2003.

Irving, Washington. *The Legend of Sleepy Hollow and Other Stories*. Easton Press, 2002.

Cerf, Phyllis and Wise, Herbert, editors. *Great Tales of Horror and the Supernatural*. Modern Library, 1994.

Poe, Edgar Allan. *Greatest Works of Edgar Allan Poe*. Fingerprint! Publishing, 2018.

Hawthorne, Nathaniel. *Twice-Told Tales*. Modern Library, 2001.

Bierce, Ambrose. *The Complete Short Stories of Ambrose Bierce*. University of Nebraska Press, 1984.

McSherry, Frank D. Jr., Waugh, Charles G., and Greenburg, Martin H., editors. *Great American Ghost Stories*. Rutledge Hill Press, 1991.

Quiroga, Horacio. *Cuentos de Amor de Locura y de Muerte*. Penguin Books, 1997.

Kaye, Marvin, compiler. *Ghosts: A Haunting Treasury of 40 Chilling Tales*. Galahad Books, 1981.

Bécquer, Gustavo Adolfo. *Rimas, Leyendas y Narraciones.* Editorial Porrúa, S. A., 1981.

Shelley, Mary. *Frankenstein.* Peter Pauper Press, 2023.

Blackwood, Algernon. *Tales of the Uncanny and Supernatural.* Spring Books, 1971.

Derleth, August (compiler). *The Best of H. P. Lovecraft.* Del Rey/Ballantine, 1982.

James, M. R. *Ghost Stories of an Antiquary.* Dover Publications, 1971.

Voltaire. *Candide.* Bantam Classics, 1983.

Davis, E. Adams. *Of the Night Wind's Telling.* University of Oklahoma Press, 1946.

Dobie, J. Frank. *Tongues of the Monte.* University of Texas Press, 1980.

Anderson, Douglas A. (editor). *Adrift on the Haunted Seas: The Best Short Stories of William Hope Hodgson.* Cold Spring Press, 2005.

Cox, Michael and Gilbert, R. A. (editors). *Victorian Ghost Stories.* Oxford University Press, 1992.

Jackson, Shirley. *The Haunting of Hill House.* Penguin Classics, 2006.

Langan, John. *The Fisherman.* Word Horde, 2016.

Ligotti, Thomas. *Songs of a Dead Dreamer and Grimscribe*. Penguin Classics, 2015.

Evenson, Brian. *A Collapse of Horses*. Coffee House Press, 2016.

Link, Kelly. *Magic for Beginners*. Small Beer Press, 2005. Saunders, George. Tenth of December. Random House, 2013.

Enríquez, Mariana. *The Dangers of Smoking in Bed*. Hogarth, 2021.

Schweblin, Samanta. *Fever Dream*. Riverhead Books, 2017.

Chiang, Ted. *Exhalation*. Alfred A. Knopf, 2019.

Machado, Carmen Maria. *Her Body and Other Parties*. Graywolf Press, 2017.

Nolan, William F. *How to Write Horror Fiction*. Writer's Digest Books, 1991.

GREYSTONE HOUSE EDITIONS

Scribere Est Sanguinare

Imprint *by Chad Harris*